GENETECH P.S

**Published by:** Blue Frog Marketing Pty Ltd
**Text Design by:** Hunter Leonard
**Cover Design by:** Hunter Leonard

National Library of Australia Cataloguing-in-Publication entry
Edition: 1st ed. October 2021

Bibliography

Subjects: Science Fiction, Fantasy Fiction

Dewey Number: 808.838
**ISBN-13: Ebook - 978-0-6452858-2-6**
**Paperback 978-0-6452858-3-3**
**Distributed by:** Blue Frog Marketing Pty Ltd

GENETECH P.S

# Genetech P.S

HUNTER LEONARD

## Note from the Author

Genetech P.S. began its life as a short story more than twenty years ago. I've always wanted to expand it into a full novel, and am delighted to present this story to you.

I've always been fascinated by the natural world and as a child collected butterflies, lizards, tadpoles, frogs - pretty much anything I could find and catch. I also frustrated my mum with all the bugs that got loose in my bedroom as a child. I reckon she was sometimes a bit scared about what she would find running loose in the room.

But the Sydney bush and plants are my first love in nature. I still love bushwalking and whilst I'm not working in a scientific field, I still have a passion for the natural world.

Having studied Botany and Land Management at Macquarie University in the early 1980's, I've always enjoyed the process of understanding plants, how they evolved, how they grow, how they survive. I was inspired by several professors at Macquarie who taught me about botany, and some of the characters have been named after them, as well as fellow students and friends.

Many of the locations in the book are real, as are some of the scientific techniques - either practically applied now, or theoretically possible in the near future.

I call this genre Science Faction. It's taking current technology and worldwide trends and dreaming of where they might lead.

If we as a human race were to be threatened with extinction - what ideas and solutions might we come up with.

I'm also interested in ethics, spirituality and philanthropy and there are elements of these subjects within the story too.

I hope you enjoy the story. I've grown quite fond of the characters whilst creating and spending time with them.

There is no doubt some of the subjects might horrify you, but whether you're inspired or scared by science, I'm hoping there will be something that makes you think, that perhaps inspires you, or makes you wonder about what might be possible.

Hunter Leonard  October 2021

# Lane Cove National Park

## Sydney Australia

## September 1983

The young girl sat hunched over her notebook. She looked up at the bush in front of her, and then back down at the paper as she sketched. She was sitting cross legged on the ground, and as she concentrated, she scrunched up her eyes and chewed on her lip.

"You coming honey?" Her mum called out from the park about 10 metres away.

"Not yet mum, i need to finish this drawing"

"Ok five more minutes and then we have to head off, it's going to pour down raining soon"

The girl hadn't even really noticed the change in the weather and temperature, but it was common in Sydney during early Spring.

"Hey mum, what do you call the green things under the flower again?" she called out.

"mmm, i think they are the CALIX" - she said.

"Oh that's right" replied the girl "thanks" she added.

She drew the word next to the drawing, pronouncing the letters out loud to herself - C.A.L.I.X. No that's not right she thought to herself. It's Y

C.A.L.Y.X

She scrubbed out the i in the word with the eraser on the end of her pencil and then drew in a Y.

She had a photographic memory, and could see the word in her mind, even though she couldn't connect that to the part of the plant always - at least not yet.

That memory helped her catalogue the names of plants and their general characteristics so she was often able to identify a plant when she saw it in the park or on a bushwalk, even though she may have only seen a photo in one of her plant books a single time.

"Marietta!, come on let's go!" her mum called again a little more impatiently.

"Ok, I'm coming" Marietta replied.

She took one more look at the drawing, satisfied she had all the parts of the bush drawn how she wanted and then stood up, stamped her feet and wiped the gum leaves off her pants as she folded the sketch book over and put the pencil in a small case.

As she got in the car, her mum said "did you draw a good one?".

"Yes, it's a Boronia Microphylla or Small Leafed Boronia" she answered, precociously giving the latin name. Most girls or boys her age would not have known this normally. In fact, unless you studied botany at university, and learnt the latin names for the genus and species of a plant, you would have thought it complete gobbledegook.

But Marietta loved the latin names, which almost always were either based on the name of the person who discovered it - telling her of it's history - for instance Banksia named for Joseph Banks - the botanist on the 1770 Captain Cook expedition of Sydney Harbour - or gave her an idea of a key feature of the plant itself. In the case of the Boronia Micro meant small and phylla meant leaf.

No normal 8 year old child knew it - but Marietta was hardly a normal young girl.

She had been obsessed with plants and animals since she was 3 or 4 years old, trailing her mum around the garden or peppering her with questions when they went to the bush or park - a favourite family pastime.

She was no doubt destined for a career in science, and while still at Primary School, had already decided she wanted to go to Macquarie University, which was just down the road from her home.

She often stood out the front of the house with her mum and watched the students with their backpacks walking in groups down the road from the university to the bushland park, chatting away amongst themselves.

She imagined herself sitting in the university looking at plants, and learning.

Unusual thoughts for an unusually gifted young girl.

Her mum was both a keen gardener and a regular bush walker, so from a very young age, Marietta had been exposed to plants and the natural world, which was no doubt part of the inspiration for her intense interest.

In any event, her early exposure to these things, would lead to a career that reached heights even Marietta couldn't dream of, as she sat in the back seat of the family car and looked at her drawing book - humming away to the music on her mum's radio.

"Hey mum - what's that song?"

"Its SWEET DREAMS by the Eurythmics" her mum said - just came out.

"I like it" Marietta said and continued humming.

**Evans Head**

**North Coast NSW**

**1990**

It was a bright and sunny winters day at Evans Head Beach. Known as the summer playground of people from inland towns like Kyogle, Casino and Lismore, Evans head was quiet at this time of the year.

The core population of locals enjoyed this time of the year when parking at the beach was simple, and the waves even better than during the busy summer.

A lone surfer paddled out from shore, lying down on his board and lazily scooping his arms through the water.

He noticed the swell building and turned his board, snapping to his feet and catching the beautiful left hander. He carved his way towards the beach as his mates looked on.

He wasn't really the usual picture of a bronzed Aussie - in fact his skin was white and his hair a flaming red. This was despite his Italian heritage. His great grand parents had come from Sicily and somewhere in his ancestry there were family members who had arrived in the region with the Normans, and even farther back there was some obvious Viking lineage to the young man.

Giacomo was in his element, despite the need for thick sunscreen, a wetsuit at all times of the year, and a broad white streak of zinc across his nose and topping his big ears.

He was a popular young teenager in Evan Head, despite his love of practical jokes, to which almost every member of the tight knit local community had succumbed at least once.

He was also a bright and diligent student, who was excelling in his studies.

Stepping into the water, off his board at the end of the wave, he leaned over, grabbed his board and walked through the shallow water to the beach.

He waved to a couple of mates watching from the shore a bit further up the beach.

After towelling himself off, he peeled off his wetsuit and changed into shorts and a t-shirt.

Leaving his board on the beach, he grabbed an old calico knapsack and walked further up the beach to the rock pools.

When he arrived, he knelt down at one of the larger pools, pulled on a face mask and put his face underwater and started observing the little ecosystem within the pool.

He had listed off over fifty different species to himself by the time the sun started dropping below the hills behind the beach.

Giacomo was particularly interested to see that certain species seemed to have their own little niche within even a small rock pool. One particular seagrass only grew on the side of the pool opposite the water. Whilst a small periwinkle only attached itself to rocks about halfway up the side of the rock pool and never at the bottom.

If you were to pick any day over the next four years; an observer would have seen what was just described to the reader.

A young red headed Aussie boy combining his twin loves of surfing and marine science.

**Casino, NSW**

**September 1992**

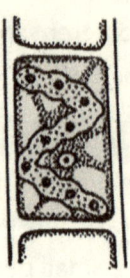

Another young man from the North Coast of NSW, and friend to Giacomo, was Damian Costa.

Hailing from a local Italian Family with several generations of history in NSW and QLD, Damian was a darker, olive complexion in contrast to his good friend.

He liked sports, but these tended more to ball sports like soccer, tennis and ping pong.

He was also a bright, intelligent young man, winning science awards right through primary and high school.

Damian's grandfather had been a wine maker - and whilst not a scientist - had understood the interaction between different life forms required to make a perfect Lambrusco. The delicate grapes of the same name, mixed with the yeast in exactly the right combination.

Hearing his grandfather talk about wine making had peaked the young man's interest in these interactions from a scientific point of view.

Damian and Giacomo's families had travelled together to Evan's Head for years, and even when Giacomo had moved permanently to the seaside town, they had remained the best of friends. They spent most weekends together exploring either the seaside rock pools or snorkelling. Or alternately, walking through the local rainforests around Kyogle, or kayaking down the local rivers and camping overnight in the bush.

It was perhaps fate when both young men were awarded scholarships to Macquarie University in late 1993, where they would continue their friendship and eventually become part of a successful scientific community as well.

**Macquarie University**

**Sydney Australia**

**February 1994**

Macquarie University is Sydney's third major university, founded in 1964. Whilst it is more than a century younger than Sydney University, it has very quickly garnered international recognition across several disciplines including a world leading MBA program, and a ranking within the top 2 per cent of universities world wide.

Set in a 126 hectare park like campus, bordering Sydney Blue Gum Bushland, Macquarie has a history of emboldened research bringing together pioneering minds and freeing them form traditional boundaries.

In 1993, three students who would both inspire and horrify the world, walked onto the campus at Macquarie for the first time.

Their journey started in an undergraduate science course and took them to the outer reaches of science and of the world.

When you first walk onto the campus early in the morning with magpies strutting around and kookaburras cackling away, it is hard to believe there are over 40000 students and 200 staff here.

But during the day at major times like morning tea or lunch, the students and staff stream out into the many cafes, and green squares dotted amongst the buildings

"Ok everyone, welcome to the start of your second year at Macquarie. I'm glad to see you made it through the first year, and transitioned to this new world of being responsible for your own timetable and study" said Professor Snow MacPherson.

A few students smiled knowingly at this comment. Macquarie was renowned for weeding out as many students as possible in 1st year with a tough introduction to after-school life.

"Ok, this subject is BIOL 201 - second year biology. This year we're going to be dealing mainly on botany, with a focus on the plants of the Sydney Basin" he added.

"Has everyone got their textbook?" he queried.

The majority of the class held up their textbook for the subject.

"Ok good, let's get on with it, and we'll start with an introduction to the different types of plant cells".

Professor Snow MacPherson was an institution at Macquarie University - and he was universally loved by all his students for his intelligent and attentive approach to teaching.

Later in life, he would become a full professor at the University of Melbourne and be known for his works in the Australian Agricultural Market.

But for now, he was at his happiest in the classrooms of second and third year botany, biology and ecology subjects at Macquarie.

Damian Costa was sitting about midway back in the lecture room - next to his mate Giacomo di Tano who was as usual spinning his pen on the top of his hands by flicking it with a finger. Damian who had tried to copy this and given up the previous year, marvelled at the nonchalant way his mate fiddled with the pen.

"Hey, stop showing off" he whispered.

"I'll stop showing off, if you stop staring at the girl in the front row" Giacomo rejoined.

"I wasn't staring" Damian said defensively.

"Oh right, sure" Giacomo said.

At which point Professor MacPherson asked - "anything to share Mr Di Tano?"

"Ummm, no Professor MacPherson"

"Ok" Snow said, half chuckling to himself - he remembered Giacomo and Damian well from first year - they were excellent students, but inclined to be talkative.

Oh well, he thought to himself - it's always the smart ones who get into trouble.

"Ok everyone" he said getting his own thoughts back to the present and his lecture room.

"Can anyone tell me what a stomata is?" Professor MacPherson asked.

The lecture continued for the next 45 mins, during which time Giacomo never stopped spinning his pen, unless he was jotting down notes.

And Damian never stopped staring at the girl in the front row.

At the end of the lecture - their final for the day and the week - Also suggested they retire to the Macquarie Bar and have a couple of beers and a game of pool or Hyperolympics.

Giacomo was addicted to the computer game, which allowed the player to compete in a range of 10 olympic events on an upright game cabinet. He'd worked out how to use a bic lighter to flick across the buttons faster than you could press with a finger - and currently held the game world record of 9.5 seconds for the hundred metres, and 3 metres for the high jump.

Damian laughed "you're going to go cross eyed playing that thing" - he personally had no interest in computer games, but agreed to a couple of beers at the bar and a game of pool.

They were in the middle of a game of pool about 20 minutes later, when a group of students walked in, grabbed drinks and stood near the pool table watching.

Damian was in the middle of a run and had pocketed 6 balls in a row, whilst Giacomo looked glumly on. "hey, take it easy, you're killing me, he said"

The boys had grown up together playing pool and ping pong and enjoyed these as a bit of down time between studies.

Damian hadn't even noticed that one of the group was the girl from the lecture hall, until Giacomo flicked him on the leg with the pool cue, and pointed this out to him in a quietly whispered comment as he walked past.

Damian immediately got distracted and shy, and missed the 8 ball shot. Giacomo was happy with this, and managed to pocket the last of his 'smalls' and the 8 ball to win the game.

Giacomo held the cue in one arm over his head like a gladiator, and downed the rest of his beer with the other. "A rare triumph for the good guy" he said.

Damian acknowledged his mate, with a toast of his own beer.

"Nicely done, enjoy it while it lasts" Damian joked.

As he turned to put the beer down, he caught the eye of the girl from the lecture and smiled shyly.

She returned the smile and walked over to him.

"Hi my name is Marietta del Pietra" she said.

"You're in my BIO 302 class, right?" she added.

"Ummm, yeah, my name is Damian" he replied.

"And my name is Giacomo" Giacomo loudly added as he wrapped his arm around Damian's shoulder and then squeezed him in a half bear hug.

"Hello" said Marietta, shaking Giacomo's hand

"How did you enjoy Snow MacPhersons first lecture" she said to them both.

"It was cool" Giacomo said

"Yeah, cool" added Damian

Usually self-confident, Damian was feeling distinctly uncomfortable standing there. Fortunately Giacomo rescued his mate, and said 'hey do you and your friends wanna join us? We are going to get a burger and I'm going to kick this guys butt at pool.

Sure said Marietta, gesturing to her friends to join them.

They all sat down at a set of lounge chairs next to the pool table, ordered drinks and chatted away for the next few hours

It was start of a friendship that would last the next thirty years. And the first of many discussions that would occur in the unofficial tutorial room of the Macquarie University Bar.

Over the following two years, Damian and Marietta were virtually inseparable, often seen walking hand in hand to lectures, working together closely on field trips.

All three graduated from their undergraduate honours degrees in 1997, and all continued on and completed masters in 2000.

They didn't stray far from their Alma Mater, all being offered research positions in the School of Biology the following year.

Giacomo pursued Marine Biology as a major with genetics as a minor and moved into research of algae and other microscopic saltwater lifeforms.

Marietta pursued double majors in Chemistry and Botany, whilst Damian majored in virology with a particular interest in the interaction between viruses and plants.

He completed his PhD thesis on the impact of viruses on commercial agriculture and kept in touch with Professor Snow MacPherson who was his masters then Phd advisor despite the latter's move to James Davis Ag College in Victoria and then to the University of Melbourne.

Snow MacPherson was a proud advocate of his three former students and also kept a close eye on the successes of Giacomo and Marietta over the years.

He was one of the first to congratulate Marietta and Damian on their engagement in 2006 and sent a case of his award winning Bimaginnie wine as an engagement present.

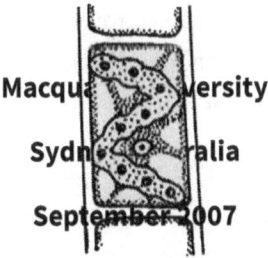

Macqua    ersity

Sydn    alia

September 2007

Associate Professor Marietta di Pietra was heading back to her lab after delivering a Biol 201 lecture in the famous main theatre of Building E7A at Macquarie University in Sydney, Australia.

The weather as usual for early autumn was still warm - in the mid 20's Celsius - and yet, the air was starting to chill in the late afternoons after another hot, humid summer that had broken records in the harbour city.

On her mind was a doctoral thesis paper she had to present on the photosynthetic attributes of a new algae they had discovered on the walls of a small fish ladder in the Lane Cove River National Park.

As she walked along the wide tree lined pathways of the Macquarie campus, she acknowledged students and smiled at fellow professors, nodding her head in greeting to a couple of grad students who worked part time in her lab.

But in reality, her mind was a million kilometres away, tossing up whether she should include the somewhat revolutionary ideas about genetically modifying simple plants for food production.

It was still bugging her when she arrived at the lab, which is why she was completely surprised when she pushed the lab door open to a loud cheer and a throng of colleagues and friends including her fiancé and fellow Associate Professor, Damian Costa. Oh, she said as she recovered from the shock - nice as it was.

Damian came over and kissed her on the cheek, handing her a piece of cake - 'We got the grant! he enthused - I can get on with the experiments now - we have enough funds to cover 3 years of work. This could revolutionise the agriculture production market in Australia and maybe globally!!"

Marietta never tired of her partners enthusiasm, and she admired his single minded passion to solve some of the emerging issues in agriculture. She particularly loved his desire to find natural solutions to problems that were currently solved by dangerous pesticides and gene shutoff techniques used by big corporations.

As fellow students, they had spent many an enjoyable day wandering various habitats around Sydney and NSW from the gum tree forests around Macquarie, to rock pools on the south coast and way out west in the dry deserts around outback Bourke.

It was near Bourke that Damian's interest in agriculture - and particularly cotton - had been sparked when he heard about the Cotton Leaf Curl Virus from Africa and Asia being found in some Australian crop locations.

Marietta congratulated Damian and his team, spending a few minutes chatting to the team and then with a plate of cake in hand, she returned to her desk to continue her "battle" with the theme for her thesis.

Three days later, something Damian said about viral transport, triggered an idea that would change not only her thesis, but the future of humanity as well.

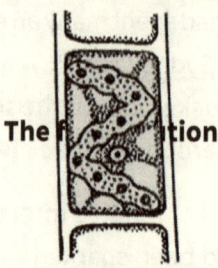

**The Revolution**

In 2019, a global research project released results that showed the population of bees - our greatest natural pollinator of food crops was in collapse.

Despite a media storm, do gooders and reality TV shows promoting home beehives plus all manner of PR stunts plus the eventual banning of the use of some toxic pesticides - eventually there was no saving the bee population in the wild

Along with the bees, a wide range of insects that also acted as pollinators had collapsed, although the bee, like the Panda became the global lightning rod of a last ditch conservation effort.

For years, toxic products like Round-up or Glyphosphate had been sold in home nurseries to consumers with no idea how incredibly damaging these products were. Incredibly, whilst banned in some forward thinking countries as potential carcinogens as well, they remained on sale in many countries for decades after this was known.

Despite living in a global economy, connected by social media and the internet, many countries stuck determinedly to their nationalistic law making - in hindsight it was supposed global corruption and pay offs kept these products on the market - but nothing was ever proven.

What was proven is that overuse of pesticides, combined with global warming amongst other factors had indeed contributed to the collapse of the global natural pollinators like bees.

Whilst food companies invested billions in ideas around mechanical harvesting and other solutions, they quickly found out there was nothing that effectively replaced insect pollination for many crops.

What the global research project didn't realise what how quickly we would be impacted - they thought decades - it turned out to be 2 years - when crops failed in the agricultural belts of Australia, Canada, the US, and China and Russia - the die was cast.

In the late 2010's, the world's population got 40% of its calories from just 3 crops, despite more than 600 being harvested for food. Groups like the World Economic Forum suggested this had to change, but unfortunately time ran out.

Grain reserves for rice, wheat and maize were tapped out, and now each years crop was being sequestered by military vehicles with massive armies patrolling all major agricultural belts around the world. Whilst crops generally did not rely on insect pollination, at 40% of the global food production, it was getting tougher to spread these crops across the globe.

Corruption and black markets were still rife, and the UN was holding on literally by its finger tips.

Major storms in parts of Europe, Queensland and the mid Western States of the USA had reduced crop yields every further.

It was described as the 'perfect storm' by media - who were always up for a trite catch phrase despite the disastrous situation.

The first deaths due to hunger occurred - as they inevitably do - in 3rd world countries - but quickly moved through wealthier countries.

One hundred million died in 2020, two hundred and fifty million in 2021.

The powerful conglomerates and wealthy individuals hoarded canned and bottled food supplies.

Major food wholesalers pushed prices to stratospheric levels until everyone was brought to heel with governments all over the world declaring martial law.

In the end, the human race found equality in starvation more than they did in human rights. Fighting broke out, but everyone soon realised that killing each other for food was insane when the lack of food was killing more people anyway.

In mid 2022, the United Nations - an organisation which had tried to hold the world together since 1947, through both investment, support and security collaboration gave up on old solutions of military intervention and food drops - these were no longer enough.

A summit was held and the UN had its charter completely revised. All shared global resources of the UN, the world bank and other organisations were re-tasked to finding solutions for global hunger, and the consequences of the deaths of nearly 5% of the world population.

After a search of global scientific literature, a reference was unearthed to an obscure PhD thesis, written by a young botanical geneticist from Australia.

And the world came calling to a small laboratory in the leafy campus of Macquarie University. A lab that would soon become the centre of efforts to save the human race from extinction.

**Whispering Pines**

**Wentworth Falls**

**Blue Mountains Region**

**February 2022**

A knock on the door of Whispering Pines startled Marietta as she was standing in the kitchen of her mountain home, staring out into the Jamison Valley.

She had been cradling a cup of lemon myrtle tea, pondering a lab problem. In the back of her mind - as always - she was also thinking about the worldwide food shortage - as many scientists were these days, since the UN announcement and request for international science support.

Australia was yet to see the worst of the global food crisis, being so distant from the rest of the world. Yet food rationing was in full swing, and most of Australia's remaining agricultural land had been swung over to expanding production so more food could be sent overseas to aid organisations.

Marietta and Damian had answered the call, and swung their own efforts back to her thesis idea of a home based, automatic food generation system.

Much like people had brewed alcohol at home during Prohibition in the USA in copper stills, Marietta had an idea to create a simple system that would allow people to use any plant based carbon source combined with a growth medium to basically turn any plant species into a food source.

She heard her husband Damian shout out from the front lounge - "I'll get it!"

She couldn't imagine who would be knocking on a Sunday here.

No one knew they were here, not even the neighbours as they had arrived very late from Sydney the previous evening.

It was early, and they'd already been out for a long walk and were now showered and dressed casually in readiness for a nice quiet Sunday in Wentworth Falls.

They always found some escape in coming to their home in the mountains.

Even though their lab was just one of hundreds like it around the world, and they were a small piece in the overall puzzle, Marietta and Damian still felt the weight of the world on their shoulders. Their sense of responsibility was in some ways out of proportion with reality, but it was what made them stretch themselves and their team to the limits.

And sometimes when you pushed hard, you need to step back to see the wood for the trees.

She heard Damian talking to someone at the door in a low voice, and she continued to stare out the windows, enjoying the scenery and not really paying any particular attention to the morning interruption.

Then she heard steps up the hallway, and as she turned saw Damian with two naval officers - a man and woman. Marietta noted that the woman had the rank of Captain whilst the man was a Lieutenant Commander.

Marietta's father had served in the Royal Australian Navy and later as a senior lecturer at the Royal Military College Duntroon in Canberra when she was in her early teens - so she knew her military ranks and badges on sight.

Marietta looked at Damian and saw a mix of concern and excitement playing across his face

Damian said - "everything's ok, but these officers want us to go with them immediately"

"Excuse me?" she answered, not really understanding the situation just yet.

"We've been asked to attend a meeting in Sydney - these officers have come from a naval helicopter that is waiting for us down at the park on Falls Road.

"What's this about? Why do we have to go now?" Marietta queried.

"We'll explain on the way" the woman said.

"It's quite urgent, we need your expertise and you've been cleared by the UN Secretary General herself"

"Oh, where are we going and how long will we be gone?"

"The answer to your first question is Sydney, but i'm afraid I can't answer the second I'm sorry. However, we can give you 10 mins to pack a bag with toiletries and a change of clothes"

"Oh, Ok" Marietta answered, and while she was somewhat perplexed at this sudden interruption to a planned day of relaxation. However, she was ever the professional and scientist and now her scientific curiosity had been well and truly piqued - why would they and their little lab be the subject of such august attention?

She left the room with Damian to pack, and within a few minutes they were ready to go. Damian sorted out locking up the house and throwing the few breakfast dishes in the dishwasher on their way out.

As they left the house, he pulled his mobile phone from his pocket and set the alarms and secure locking of the downstairs lab and office. He also secured the home internet and other communications diverting all calls to his phone. Finally, he set the home on 'absent' mode which would program the lights, window shutters to randomly turn on and off, open and close to look like someone was home.

Not that it was absolutely necessary here in the quiet suburb of Wentworth Falls but there was a lot of confidential data down in the lab, and he preferred to reduce the risk as much as possible.

Little did they know, they wouldn't be back for nearly six months.

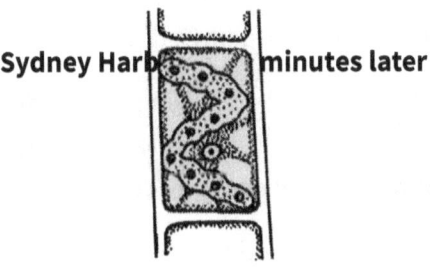

Sydney Harb **minutes later**

Flying at close to its top speed of 300 km/h, the trip in the NH90 helicopter took just a little over 20 minutes. A bit faster than the 100 kilometre drive they'd done quite a few times down the Blue Mountains Highway onto the M4 and then Parramatta Road into the city, Damian mused to himself.

The Helicopter had flown in from the west, straight over Parramatta and then following the Parramatta River through to the harbour before heading almost directly over the centre of the iconic Sydney Harbour Bridge and Sydney Opera House, slowing down as it did so.

A little too quick fast for Marietta's liking, who wasn't a good flyer at the best of times - let alone in a super fast, stripped down military helicopter that wasn't really built for comfort.

The helicopter began descending down to the deck of a large ship docked at Garden Island. Damian could see it was carrying the red ensign of the Royal Australian Navy, but he didn't recognise the ship.

"What ship are we landing on?" he asked, as he pressed up against the small window next to his seat. Unlike Marietta, Damian loved flying - and was happy in anything from an Airbus A380 down to a single engine Cessna.

He had even flown in a tiny gyrocopter whilst surveying a beech forest in Tasmania. It had just two seats, and the floor was see through plastic. He remembered hovering just a couple of feet above 300 foot tall forest trees, taking photos of the canopy of the forest.

"She's the flagship of the RAN", lieutenant commander Peters answered, bringing Damian back to the present.

The two officers - Browning and Davis, still hadn't given first names, and were pretty much silent on the ride from the Blue Mountains, other than briefly telling them why they had been summoned in such a rush.

"She carries the name HMS Canberra, displaces 27,500 tonnes at full load, can travel at up to 20 knots, and carries a full ship company of 360 personnel. She carries up to 110 vehicles on her two decks, and up to 6 helos with the ability to rapidly deploy 220 soldiers by airlift"

"Ok, thanks - Damian was a bit of a geek, and was impressed by the knowledge of the commander, even though he wasn't that interested in the war capabilities of the ship. He was a pacifist at heart, like most non military scientists.

The helicopter touched down, and the commander slid back the main door, gesturing for them to disembark, motioning to them to keep their heads down as they got off and moved away from the aircraft.

When they were clear of the rotors, and away from the noise, the commander asked them to follow him towards the main superstructure of the ship.

They entered a hatchway, and walked down a series of corridors and stairs - each looking the same to Damian and Marietta - until they came to a briefing room door. There were two MP's on duty outside the door.

The Commander said "I'll leave you here - everything else will be explained inside this room"

"You're not coming with us?" Marietta asked.

"No, I'm not cleared for this meeting - the MP's will show you in" He said - smiling briefly and then turning on his heels and heading back the way he came.

One of the MP's asked them for identification, which seemed a little over the top to both of them, but they pulled out their drivers licenses and stood their whilst the MP compared them to their photos.

Marietta laughed, and said "I wasn't allowed to smile, so I look like a bit of a criminal in that photo"

The MP didn't react at all to that, handing back the licenses and then opening the door.

"Thank you ma'am, thank you sir"

They entered the room, and were somewhat shocked to see both the Prime Minister, the Governor General, and the Chief of the Defence Force in the room, with some other people they didn't know.

Most shocking of all was that the President of the United States and his entourage were also in the room.

A woman stood up, and motioned them to the two chairs that were vacant at the large conference table.

She introduced herself - "my name is Angelique Charpentier, I am a representative of the UN secretary general, and charged with bringing together a team to handle the current worldwide food crisis"

"I can see from the expression on your faces you recognise some of the important people in this room, including your Prime Minister and the President of the United States"

"The others will introduce themselves as we go on, but I'm sure you are wondering why you are here in this room"

"Well to put it mildly yes, Marietta answered as Damian nodded in agreement"

Angelique continued "we have been asked to sequester you and to take charge of your research team and projects, moving them under military control as of 8am this morning."

"Whaat! Damian blurted! You can't do that, we're working on some important ideas for food production and we're close to a solution that may actually solve this problem - at least in the short term."

"Yes we understand Professor Costa, but please don't worry - this is for your protection rather than some other nefarious military reason"

"Oh, and why do we need that?" Marietta inquired, crossing her arms defensively across her chest.

"Please, allow me to turn this over to the Prime Minister to explain" Angelique said calmly and Marietta decided she liked her immediately and sat back and gestured to continue.

"Professor Costa - ummm - Marietta, may I call you by your first name? "

The Prime Minister began.

"Sure she answered, it might be easier since we are both Professor Costa"

"Your work has come to our attention, after your presentation at the UN summit earlier this year" he explained.

"In consultation with the President - who was here for his first trip to Australia, since being elected, we decided to ask you along to explain things first and to seek your opinion on the potential for success"

"We're not scientists, and we thought a short explanation might be useful  before we get you along to the rest of your team at the Quarantine Station in North Head"

"Where?!, Damian interrupted once again.

"We're moving your team to a secure location, where they will be guarded 24 hours a day for the next period of time by military personnel from Australia and the US.

"Why do we need protection?"

Angelique answered this one "if I may sir, this week there have been attacks on several other labs around the world from people opposed to science being the solution"

"You see" Angelique continued "Even though there are hundreds of labs working the problem, we have our own rating system on those projects, and there were perhaps less than 8 that have a real chance of a solution that is scalable enough to handle the problem" She said

"And your's is now the only one of those 8 that is still operational - the head scientists of the other 7 were killed on those attacks - we suspect someone has leaked our ratings system and they know which ones are likely of success - given time"

The President nodded, and added - "ma'am our combined military team will be honoured to protect your team whilst you finalise this important work - if it's going to work that is? He enquired.

Marietta nodded "well thank you I think - it's a bit of a shock to be honest - we just left the lab yesterday and this is a bit sudden"

"Well will it work?", the Prime Minister asked somewhat impatiently - he wasn't known for his patience - that much was obvious since he came to power late the previous year.

Marietta said "we really think it will, but there's a lot of work to be done, potentially two to three years of testing and trials, but to answer your question, Yes, we're confident it will work if we can solve the medium and growth issues.

"You have six months" - the Prime Minister said

"Impossible!" Damian stood up and added "it's a precise piece of work, we couldn't speed it up that much with the resources we have - our team is quite small and we only have enough funding for…

"Yes, Yes I understand Damian" the Prime Minister interjected, "but please don't concern yourself with worries about resources."

"The UN and the USA have generously committed resources in the form of scientists and anything else you need - you now have effectively unlimited support, yet limited time - can you achieve what we need under those conditions?" he added.

"Oh, well in that case, probably" Damian sat back down - mollified but thoughtful - "We'll have to work on a schedule for you over the next few days and then confirm but it's doable" "sorry" he added as an afterthought - "we're used to working under university conditions" - he laughed and the rest of the room joined him as the tension was relieved - for the moment anyway.

The President then added - "perhaps we could have that explanation now? And if possible in plain english, I'm a simple man, and I never did well in science"

"Sure" said Marietta and for the next 20 minutes she expertly yet simply explained their idea of a portable home food production engine.

She covered the construction of the solar powered engine, the theory of the growth medium - explaining what they had not yet solved.

She gave them a briefing on genetics and GMO and how they planned to breed the super 'plant' that would provide the food. Using ginger beer as an analogy she explained the concept of a 'plant' that worked as a starter for a drink like ginger beer and how the same concept could be used to program a food production system.

"In summary, we have three major parts to the problem - the first is the source vegetable based carbon and how to process it for things like poisons, cellulose and so forth, the second is the growth medium, and the third is how to make the whole system simple enough for any person, anywhere in the world, to use it and robust enough to last several years without any maintenance whatsoever" Marietta concluded her presentation.

The prime minister looked over at his fellow leader and both men nodded.

"Ok, thank you for explaining Professor, I won't pretend I understand the process of solving it, but as a concept I get what you're trying to do" He said and then added

"I'm a authorised by the UN to let you know you now have full approval to proceed as of this moment, and Angelique will be your main contact" The President added.

"We won't be meeting again face to face" The Prime Minister said.

"Oh!, queried Damian"

"Yes, in fact this meeting never happened - we want to keep this last allocation of military and scientific support as quiet as we can to buy you time" The Prime Minister said.

"And we" he added, indicating the President and himself "have a lot of other population and food management crisis to attend to, whilst you get on with your task"

"Angelique, we will leave you to sort out the details, shall we?" concluded the President.

And with that all the politicians and their aides left the room, leaving Marietta and Damian alone with Angelique.

"Well that's settled - Angelique said - it falls to me to be your liaison with the UN.

"We'll have the Navy fly you direct from here to the North Head Quarantine station so you can begin getting the lab sorted with your team and get back to work immediately"

"This is going to take more than a few days" Damian said, referring to the comments from the naval personnel.

"Yes, it will" Angelique said "I'm sorry for the less than complete information the naval personnel were able to provide, but they were operating with all the information we gave them and we wanted to ensure you got a full briefing before understanding the situation we were putting you in.

"We'll have to get back to the house in the next couple of days to secure it for a longer term" Damian added.

Angelique replied - "Unfortunately we will have to send a naval personnel and a helicopter up to do what you need. As the station is under military security, we'll want you to stay at the station for the time being - would that be ok"

"Yes, I suppose so, ok fine" Damian replied. Although he was thinking to himself he was bummed about missing the walks and environment around their escape pad in the Mountains.

"Ok, hon, let's get going then" Marietta added, with a knowing look at her husband and a barely perceptible nod to let him know she understood exactly what he was thinking.

Once they were aboard the helicopter, the pilot cycled the propellers up to speed and lifted the aircraft off the deck of the HMS Canberra.

He then turned north east and flying directly up the harbour towards the famous Sydney Harbour Heads and landed just a couple of minutes later at the North Head Quarantine station.

For the many tourists who have visited Sydney by cruise ship, North Head is to the right as they enter the world's most beautiful harbour.

It is covered by thick heathland bush - a mix of flannel flowers, heath banksia, grass trees, boronia and coastal tea-trees. The tea trees were so named for the often deep brown tea coloured water found where these trees grew near small creeks and streams.

This 'tea-coloured' water comes from the tannin found in the leaves of these trees.

The wildlife is a spectacular mix of reptiles, birds and insects.

The cheeky and territorial Eastern Water Dragon is a perennial favourite with tourists often cadging a piece of apple or other snack from walkers taking a break on the sandstone rocks.

In the early mornings, especially near the hanging swamps and on overcast spring days, visitors are serenaded by a surprisingly loud crick-crick-crick from the Common Eastern Froglet which grows to only about 3cm in length but sings at a volume that belies its small stature.

On rare occasions, you can be fortunate to spot a Long-Nosed Bandicoot.

Usually active at night, it is occasionally caught "on the hop" in the headlights of cars, returning to its burrow in the morning or heading out early in the winter evenings to forage for insects.

New Holland Honeyeaters dodge from flower to flower and are a common sight, along with little wattlebirds who use their long brush-tipped tongue to probe for nectar in flowers.

The Sanctuary is a popular walk for locals and tourists alike, with many phenomenal viewing platforms looking back into the harbour, across to middle and south heads and out to sea.

The Manly Ferry could often be seen toiling its way back and forth between Circular Quay and Manly Beach.

On some days, the ferry leans almost sideways battling the large swell that comes up in rough weather at the opening to the harbour.

The distinctive yellow and green ferries are a key part of the public transport system of the harbourside city, but equally an amazing opportunity for tourists to see the harbour from the water. And all for just a few dollars.

Before the white occupation of Australia began in 1788, the aboriginals used North Head for gatherings and medicinal practices, which made a interesting yet poignant comparison to the later uses of North Head as a quarantine station for ships arriving to the colony between 1828 and 1879.

In the early 1800's there was little recognition of the advanced levels of culture and knowledge of the Aboriginal tribes who had been custodians of the land around Sydney Harbour for the better part of forty thousand years - an almost imaginable time period - almost two hundred times the length of white civilisation.

And yet the aboriginals had lived in harmony with the natural environment for the entirety of that time, such that Sydney Harbour was an unspoilt paradise and wilderness for plants and animals - despite the newly arrived Europeans describing it as hostile to the colonists way of life.

The new white colony of Sydney almost didn't survive ten years, let alone 40000.

During the early 1900's the newly minted Commonwealth of Australia took over responsibility for quarantine duties at North

Head and in World War Two, the North Head station became a key part of Australia's harbour defence strategy.

In 1946 the school of artillery was established on the station and it only closed in 1998.

In the early 2000's the Harbour Trust took over responsibility for the whole reserve and this was the last time it was used for anything other than public recreation, which began in 2007 when the North Head Sanctuary opened to the public.

In a little known fact, the military actually maintains a small underground base in the Sanctuary - as a listening post for ships passing the harbour and to co-ordinate communications with naval personnel and ships leaving and entering the harbour.

This secret installation is reached through a labyrinth of tunnels and locked doors from within the old barracks and from below old gun emplacements, where ingeniously weighted concrete platforms could be cycled open to allow entry and exit and close without any sign that there is an operational base nearby and below the old world war concrete gun emplacements.

The North Head Sanctuary had been closed a week or so before Marietta and Damian's team was moved there, allowing the military time to clean up and commission old barracks for sleeping, set up the basics of equipment for a base hospital and prepare the fundamentals for research labs.

This was done with typical efficiency by The Royal Australian Corps of Engineers and when the team arrived, there was a good foundation for them to add their own technical expertise for specialised experiments that they would be conducting over the next few months.

Whilst the Harbour Trust was informed of the closure, they were not informed of the specific usage of the facilities which was on a need to know basis.

Interestingly enough, the trust itself had for many years called for proposals from health, well-being and environmental research groups to adapt and use the facilities. So perhaps they would have been interested to know what it was about to be used for.

Given the medicinal use by the aboriginals, the quarantine background, the requests from the trust, and the now secret and critical work now to be done by Marietta and Damian it was almost as if fate had chosen the site for them.

Fate would have other ideas in the coming months.

**The first solution explained.**

"Ok everyone, let's get started" Marietta said as she called the small group meeting to order.

Her lab team was settled into a small conference room adjacent to the labs - it was an old building, but well appointed with new carpet, and a large display screen on one wall.

Although the table and chairs were old, they were comfortable and in the centre of the table, there was a large round speaker phone and a camera connected to the top of the TV completed the set up for conference calls with Angelique in the UN, which would be conducted daily by Marietta and Damian, once all daily progress reports were entered into the project tracking system.

Each individual scientist used a private and secure document, video and audio storage system and recorded their reports into an equally secure and private app modelled on REV - a commercially available audio transcription service used by business people around the world.

All the scientist had to do was dictate their daily findings and progress and it would be transcribed automatically by the AI engine driving the app. Reports were then automatically updated into the online storage where they could be accessed by team leaders and of course the UN.

A simple traffic light master report was collated from all individual reports and available to Marietta and Damian to review at any time.

Each evening the group got together to share their results and discuss next steps in a team dinner and meeting.

They had found this system had worked well in their old lab - where all of these systems had been paper based. Now will virtually unlimited resources, they had been able to take advantage of the latest in communications and reporting technology used by the armed forces and government departments.

Marietta began "Well I know it's been a but of a whirlwind few days in set up, and you've all been yanked from your normal day to day lives, for which I'm sorry, but we have been tasked with an important project and I'm very glad you're all here to participate"

There was nodding all around the table, a few people in the team looked a big jaded and tired but no wonder given the accelerated set up of the new labs and long days stretching into late evenings and early mornings.

"We hope you're comfortable and I understand some of you have some concerns and issues, but if I may, can I ask you to hold those individual things to be handled offline as I really want to focus this first meeting on re-setting our overall project goals now we have all these new toys and resources to facilitate our project"

At that, everyone brightened a little - there wasn't a scientist alive who didn't like the idea of having new toys to play with in the lab - whether it was a new microscope, or liquid chromatography machine. It brought out the kid in most of them, albeit a big kid, with an IQ north of 150 in most cases.

"Ok, so I'll hand over to Giacomo, who will be handling day to day operations of the lab teams and co-ordinating your efforts - Giacomo?"

Giacomo stood up and went over to the display, turning on his iPad at the same time. It was linked to the external display so he could map out processes and systems in a sketch program as they discussed.

Once again, any hand sketches were then automatically turned into project diagrams with milestones and tracking once the team agreed.

"Let's start with the prototype food production unit, Peter? WIth your new engineering lab, what are your thoughts on timing and requirements?"

Peter Davis, the teams scientific instrument engineer said "oh, I reckon we can have a dozen prototype units ready within a couple of weeks - having access to the titanium for the casing, and also the rare elements to be used in the hardware, I'm pretty confident in bringing forward our old plans by at least 2-3 months"

"Thats great Peter, thank you for the update" Giacomo said.

A good start, but the mechanics were the least of their problems Giacomo thought to himself - it was incredibly important to have a robust production unit, but with no ingredients it would be as useful as dinghy anchor on a cruise ship.

"Moving on, where are we at with the algae selection" He asked Dave Craig - their field scientist.

"We've collected about a dozen local species and had another hundred or so flown in from various organisations around the world who are contributing their IP to the project" Dave replied.

"Our current thinking is that lead candidates will come from the existing commercially available species like Spirulina from Cyanotech or perhaps Nannochloropsis from Qualitas Health.

In a rare showing of corporate collaboration, several organisations worldwide had agreed to share algal culture material with the project.

Whilst many of these companies were leaders in the premium health food markets of the developed nations, they didn't have an interest or capacity to take on worldwide distribution of a low cost food production for the entire global population.

Algae has long been identified as a potential source of protein - with some species rivalling meat, egg, soybean and milk for protein content.

Marine Algae in particular has been a priority candidate because it's production didn't require more freshwater, already stretched due to other food production.

But with the collapse of grain crops, and a subsequent decimation of meat producing herds around the world, the selection table was open to include freshwater algae as well.

The difficulty has been in extracting the protein with various methods being used including chemical and ultrasound extraction.

Many of these companies were on the brink of collapse anyway, as world demand for premium products collapsed as people diverted their own resources in procuring the simple necessities. No one had time for wellness products, when they had enough trouble just surviving.

Some companies who had already filed for liquidation had had their IP purchased in fire sales by the World Bank and this IP was contributed to the project.

Others who were initially unwilling, were convinced when they realised the extent of the worldwide problem.

A few companies held out for a government contribution for their IP, but most shared it openly and freely.

"Ok, that's great" said Giacomo "can you keep us in the loop on the local species as well - it may prove to be easier to harvest more for experiments if the feed cultures sent from overseas run out, it's going to be tough to get more in a hurry"

"Also, I want us to be aware of the potential for certain species and survival in different temperatures, elevations, humidity and so forth around the world - we may indeed need different algae for different climates" Giacomo said.

"Ok, no worries" said Dave - we're on it.

"And while you're at it, can you grow us up a supply of that Red Dulse that tastes like bacon when you fry it - if I can't have bacon, I'll settle for something that tastes like it?" Said Giacomo, who was as always partial to his food, and was missing a morning hit of eggs and bacon - his favourite breakfast.

There were quite a few chuckles at this around the table.

"mmm, not sure about that" Dave replied

"No worries Dave, just kidding with you, awesome as always mate - continue on"

"Next is Damians pet zoo - the Tardigrades" mused Giacomo, still in a mood to create a little mischief to relieve the tension in the room.

"Hey don't diss my water bears" said Damian.

"They look more like mini sumo's to me" Giacomo said laughing.

"Well they might just be the answer to our biggest problem - transport" said Damian.

"If you can only get them to sit still long enough to take a genetic sample" Giacomo persisted.

"Ok, Ok" Damian held up his hands in a gesture of defeat.

"Sorry, continue on" said Giacomo - who knew it was time to move on to the serious stuff again.

Damian explained that they had over 600 species already collected and they were in the process of sampling each to check DNA compatibility and survival in extreme conditions.

Tardigrades - a near microscopic animal were often called water bears, because this is roughly what they looked like under a microscope. They also looked a little like they were wrapped up in one of those blow up sumo wrestling suits you sometimes saw at carnivals and in comedy movies. The difference being they had what looked like a scrunched up face with a massive hose shaped "nose" on front and no eyes.

These tiny animals - also called moss piglets - after one of the habitats they lived in, are one of the most amazing creatures on our planet. They are virtually indestructible and can go into a semi hibernation state and survive exposure to outer space.

Damian had been considering the hypothesis that using some of the tardigrade genes inserted into the algae might give it the ability to survive being dried out for transport in the food production 'feed' kit - massively reducing the hassles and issues of transport.

"Like Dave, we have a few lead candidates - these are the species that are found in the most extreme habitats around the world" Damian continued.

"Ramazzottius saltensis or Ramazzottius montivagus are right up there in terms of long term survival without water. There's a science team at the University of Edinburgh's Institute of evolutionary biology that have been waking up Tardigrades each year for the last couple of decades" Damian added.

"You say tomato, I say toh-may-to" interjected Giacomo - who despite his humour, loved rolling the latin names of various animals across his tongue - in fact he had a small note book of his favourite all time latin plant and animal names - lovingly collected over many years like some people collect favourite words.

"Anyway" Damian continued without allowing Giacomo to disrupt him too much - it was a banter that had been going on for near on 30 years.

"We'll know more next week, when the rest of the samples arrive, I'm particularly confident about those ones because they actually co-exist with algae in their preferred habitats and at that microscopic level, we've often seen genetic harmony between co-habiting species - we might see less chance of rejection' he concluded.

"Ok" Giacomo concluded - "that wraps up this review, lets call it a day there, and pick up on the scaling algal populations tomorrow"

And with that, the team headed back to their individual projects and assignments.

Prior to Damian's idea about Tardigrades, there was discussion of growing cultures of algae and sending them alive in similar tanks to those used to move live fish around the world. They even had some sample tanks already in the loading bay from a company named Fishpac in Melbourne - a leader in safe transport of live fish.

But when someone did the maths on the exercise they realised they effectively needed one tank per family and even if they could produce them they would then need literally millions of 747 cargo plane flights or thousands of cargo ships with millions of containers to achieve the necessary distribution of tanks.

By contrast, drying out or desiccating the algae and then only adding the amount required to make up food for a day or two, was a far superior method of getting the food production unit and supplies around the globe.

Of course production of units would be carried out in locations around the globe, but there were only a half dozen or so commercial scale algae production zones that could be used, so at least the algae had to be transported from there to continental distribution points where fleets of trains and trucks could get it to regional and local destinations along with locally produced food production units as directed by the UN.

The main part of the food production unit itself looked very similar to a large pressure cooker. It could be connected to normal electricity of any voltage with a built in converter.

The unit had one simple dial which measured the bulking up of the algae protein in the unit - when it hit 100% the process was done.

The unit had a water storage tank much like a large coffee pod machine, which could be filled with either fresh or salt water -

through a filtration system, the unit removed salt and and high temperature coil destroyed any microbes in the water on one pass.

When Marietta's and Damian's team solved the starter ingredients pack, it would be in simple packages with a biodegradable seaweed packaging that could be thrown into the unit with the water leaving zero waste.

Further seaweed sachets with flavouring could be added to the first. These flavour packs had already been researched and perfected by a global spice company, and had just been about to be launched when the crisis struck. The company generously donated all its flavour research and its production facilities and was even now cranking out the flavour sachets in advance of a breakthrough from the team on the algae protein base.

# Growing the Algae

Any child who has tried it, knows that it is a relatively simple exercise to cultivate algae - even at home - much like in hydroponic gardens. All that is needed is purified fresh or saltwater depending on the species of algae. Also some plastic tubing, a tank, some nutrients and a pure culture of the chosen algae.

Scientists usually culture their preferred algae on agar plates - a gelatinous product that is put in small round glass trays and which have been used for years to test the effectiveness of antibiotics against bacteria and disease.

They seed the algae onto the agar plate and it will multiply into a visible colony. They then ensure the colony is a pure single species and will transfer this into their scaling tanks.

School kids are often shown how to start from a clear plastic or glass container filled with sterilised saltwater, although Spirulina requires freshwater.

Boiling the water first removes most contaminants.

The clear glass or plastic allows sunlight to get to the algae.

Algae require some nutrients and these can be provided by a commercial nutrient solution or simply adding a little pond water or fish tank water.

Algae can often be collected from a river, dam, rock pool or other body of water or to be more precise a starter culture from a scientific supplier - which is often considered to be the best approach for a food product like Spirulina.

After seeding the water with the algae, it is placed in the sun, and monitored for the colour change as the colony grows, nutrient levels and so forth.

The process used by the research team wasn't much more complex than this, albeit a little more controlled. And of course they were looking to genetically modify the algae and other organisms to be used for worldwide food production, so the stakes were a lot higher than the usual science fair experiment.

## Once a Tardigrade

"Ok, now carefully inject the sample into the algae cell" Damian said as he oversaw the lab assistants work.

On the screen, a small needle like instrument was moving towards what looked like a small green balloon.

It reached the edge of the balloon, pushed inwards and pierced the cell wall. The two scientists then saw a small puff of liquid move from the needle into the cell.

In reality, the needle was just a half micron in diameter - or about one thirtieth the thickness of a human hair.

"Ok, great, now just repeat that 100 times and you've got yourself a sample" Damian said.

"Thanks" said the lab assistant - I was having trouble keeping the pipette steady, so understanding where to place the micro manipulators was useful" he said.

"No worries, keep me in the loop on your progress" Damian said as he moved off down the lab benches to check on the rest of the team.

They were now into the full scale testing of all the algae samples and the tardigrade gene injections, having selected the final candidates from both microscopic life forms.

Damian had on occasion wondered if these lifeforms were at some level 'conscious' of their surroundings and what they would make of these huge instruments coming into their environment.

They had often joked at University about what would happen if humans found themselves under some cosmic microscope with huge beings testing and prodding them. A joke that had been deftly communicated by science fiction writers like Phillip Dick in the mid 20th Century.

He pushed this thought aside and engaged with the next lab assistant to see how they were progressing on their experiment.

At the end of his lab tour, he caught up with Giacomo and Marietta to discuss the process of gene splicing and introduction of the tardigrade DNA.

They also dialled in Angelique from the UN to give her an update at the same time.

"I guess my first question is how do we know which genes are expressing for the ability to survive desiccation? Angelique asked when the basic briefing was over.

"Without a gene map that has been sequenced to the physical expression in each species, it would be incredibly difficult" said Giacomo.

"But fortunately we have all the species of the Tardigrade and in testing, we've been able to isolate a specific gene sequence, which appears in those tardigrades which are in more extreme environments, but has been lost or isn't expressed in those that live in easier environs"

"And of course our task is also made easier through the use of the Artificial Intelligence(AI) program we were gifted by the Israelis." he added

"And how is it, you know, cut out?" Angelique asked.

"Well we've advanced a great deal in the last twenty years in the genetics field" Giacomo said.

"We start by tracking the genes using MRNA, and then we can add, cut out, modify genes, even down to a single base pair.

"In this case, we're selected 12 base pairs in a specific sequence in the tardigrade, which we are removing by gene lysis and then we're using a viral vector to get those base pairs into the algae cell, where the viral vector will ensure it gets encoded into the host DNA."

"Then it's a simple matter of breeding and refining down around 100 generations of the algae and we'll have a new species we can use to grow for our food source - one that theoretically will survive the desiccation(drying) process and be able to come alive again when water is added again"

"100 generations!!!! Angelique said - how long is that going to take?"

"Ah, not to worry" Giacomo answered. "Most of the algae were looking at reproduce asexually and divide like wildfire. With 5 days of the final selection, we'll have 'technically speaking' the hundredth generation of the plant growing in our tanks.

Chances are, Damian and Marietta won't be waiting for me! I'll be sitting on the beach sipping Pina Coladas with my work done, well before they get your act together"

Now is was Damian's turn to laugh wryly.

"Challenge accepted" he chuckled and held out his hand to Giacomo to shake on the bet.

"Ok, well that's all the information I need" said Angelique, slightly bemused at the byplay of the two crazy Aussies, whom she had grown fond of in the last few weeks.

She saw that they were dedicated to their task and progressing well, and that their way of letting off steam was a healthy indicator of a strong team culture.

Angelique had worked with several Australians at the UN over the years, from interpreters to her close friend and fellow team member - Nicole Doherty - who was head of the Community Partnerships Directorate at the UN. She had noticed they all shared this same laconic and less than serious style - but Australians were known for their ingenuity and inventiveness too.

Necessity is the mother of invention was a phrase she was reminded of. A culture that had grown out of a mix of pioneering and convicts. It just went to show that other old phrase that 'man is most himself when he achieves the seriousness of a child at play'.

Damian and Giacomo certainly embodied that principle that good things got done and that just because a situation was serious didn't mean you had to approach it seriously.

The three friends and work colleagues then continued talking through some of the logistics of the work to select the algae and Tardigrade combination to be used in the commercial production stage.

# First Success

With a flourish, Giacomo slipped the small bottle of champagne out of his backpack and handed it to Marietta.

The bottle was labelled as containing Domaine Chandon - an Australian made sparkling wine - which technically couldn't be called champagne but everyone did anyway.

Marietta held it in her hands and smiled briefly before holding it up in the air and the rest of the team cheered.

They wouldn't be drinking this, but Marietta had smiled at the suggestion of Giacomo to smash it against the box of the first prototype food unit. That unit was now awaiting loading onto the Helicopter ready for transport to the first commercial production factory in Indonesia.

From there several first run units would be made and then sent on to other production facilities on each continent. These facilities had already brought in supplies of steel, electronics and other materials ready to produce based on the technical CAD drawings which were also about to be sent.

A prototype unit was needed in the factory to compare drawings to the actual unit as a quality standard. This would prevent any translation errors and ensure each unit compared to the original in every detail.

Of particular note was the material that Peter Davis had used for the seals - it was neither rubber nor silicone - in fact it was an invention of his own - Algicone - which could be made easily from the same algae they were using as the source plant. Simply by taking one seaweed sachet of the source plant and adding unfiltered salt water the algae went into a semi-hibernation state and produced a soft, pliable 'skin' on its external surfaces.

This skin turned out to be an effective seal on the food production unit, and since it could be replaced simply, on the ground by the operator - it was superior to using rubber or silicone seals that required specialised manufacturing techniques.

Marietta smiled again when she found the bottle of champagne was actually filled with bath crystals and made out of plastic - so there would be no smashing it against the unit - so she tapped it lightly on the box, whilst saying theatrically - 'tada!' and everyone cheered again.

They were all standing out in a circle around a small composite plastic sled, onto which the unit was packed and wrapped in a thick plastic like glad wrap. Around the sled and plastic was a webbed harness, which was connected to a steel cleat to which a steel cable was connected to the waiting helicopter.

One of the engineer corp check the cleat and harness one last time, and then stepped aside to give a thumbs up to the pilot.

The team stepped back a few paces and whilst everyone watched it lifted off and headed out to sea to the US Naval transport which would steam north with its precious cargo to Indonesia over the next few days.

In the next few months, the world witnessed a modern manufacturing miracle as multiple factories came on stream and began producing millions and then tens of millions of units per day.

It was as much a distribution miracle too, as ships and trucks left these facilities 24 hours a day headed to every local region in each country.

Long lines were inevitable at distribution points because each person or family needed to be given a unit and some simple instructions on set up.

These instructions were of course repeated in a small plaque on each unit, but a physical demonstration of the unit along with short 'explainer' videos posted on every social media and news site around the globe were useful additions to ensure each person would actually be able to use and maintain the unit to make their own food.

Military personnel were present at each dispatch location around the world, but perhaps surprisingly as soon as the populace realised there was no shortage of units or food sachets, there was very little violence or upset.

Healthcare professionals provided emergency care for anyone who was malnourished in the wait for the units providing bolus nutrient injections and in some cases, larger commercial versions of the units had been produced first and sent to extreme locations where the worst hunger and loss of life had occurred in order to save as many people as possible.

Within 6 months, every single village, town and city on the planet had been supplied with units and source food sachets.

The first solution was an unqualified triumph for the human race in terms of co-operation and survival.

Death due to starvation dropped to almost zero - improved even on what used to be thought of as normal back in the early part of the 21st Century.

The face of that unqualified success was Marietta Costa, and it was to her that the world turned to say thanks - in the form of a Nobel Prize which was awarded that December in Stockholm.

**Stockholm, Sweden**
**10 December, 2022**

OMG! Can you believe it babe?

Damian was still walking on air after attending what was a life changing event - the presentation of a Nobel Prize for chemistry to Marietta for her work on designing the in-home food production unit now feeding the world's populations.

In the months following the collapse of the world's main agricultural zones due to a rapidly accelerating climate change, and the death of 99% of the world's bee population, Marietta and her team had accelerated the development of a concept using genetically modified cross bred organism, which had elements of bacteria, mould and algae.

The end result was a desiccated powder that could be programmed to produce over a thousand times its weight in food from water and any carbon based matter. It kept reproducing and turning this matter into an amino acid, protein and carbohydrate super food that could be programmed to resemble anything from bread to steak to vegetables - it actually could even be made to 'taste like chicken' - that last point had nearly brought the house down when Marietta had mentioned it in her acceptance speech.

The prize was now hanging around her neck, as they walked the park near the Stockholm City Hall, enjoying the cool of an early winter evening.

The Stadshusparken or Sculpture Park between the city hall and the shore of Lake Malaren was beautiful in the late evening, and many of the sculptures were lit upwards giving the park and ethereal feeling, especially given the light mist that had rolled in. It reminded Damian of the Norman Lindsay Sculptures near their home in the

Blue Mountains - although the two places could not have been further removed in style.

Just like she had done many years ago on the University Campus, Marietta acknowledged other guests as they passed by, only this time, the awe in which she was held was adding to the palpable energy in the air.

You did it!

Yes babe, we did it, but the job is only partly done, when we run out of the growth mediums and we will, it will all start again"

Marietta answered, excited by the achievement but at the same time still dissatisfied in the way only scientists are when the problem remains unsolved.

She turned around and lent back against the stone wall in front of one fo the sculptures, feeling the chill of the stone through her evening coat.

"I just don't see us touching lightning twice"

"Nope, I'm confident we'll solve it again", Damian enthused. "And what about the viral transport idea - we've still got that"

The prize had been swiftly bestowed - the fastest award in history - it had only been 3 months since the first units were sent to Africa, Asia and South America.

The invention was being credited with saving the human race, although nearly half a billion had starved in the months that it took to crack the production and transport issues of the growth medium and the GMO organism.

The protests from people worried about GMO have been swiftly submerged in the rush by world governments to order units as their emergency reserves food supplies dwindled.

Marietta smiled, because the award around her neck could have been a Peace prize and they would be standing in Norway, not Stockholm, for all the arguments and near fights she had averted.

In her calm manner dealing with heads of state and ambassadors who would turn up at her door will all sorts of offers to jump the queue - but in the end Marietta had won out.

She had delivered the orders in exactly the reverse order of countries GDP per capita - reasoning that the richer countries could afford their own short term solutions for longer - and her  strategy had proven out.

Who would have thought that including just 12 gene pairs from a Tardigrade and snap freezing the organism would be the answer - that one had come from Damian - with his passion for the weird and wonderful of the natural world - he was a botanist, but his interests spilled over into the microscopic world of animals too.

Damian had been the one to recognise the potential of the Tardigrade due to its ability to survive extreme environments - even the depths of space - in a semi-animate state. He'd also been the one to collect almost all of the 1100 or so species of Tardigrade from around the world, and putting them through an AI search for the right gene sequence for their project.

Marietta's mind started clicking over, faster and faster - as it always did when she was searching for a solution.

And while she was at the party, and guests would testify to the fact - in reality, she was already preparing for the future push to a complete and total solution - taking genetic modification to a level never dreamed of, nor countenanced by any sane person on the planet - at least before the seriousness of this situation.

"But they'll never allow it - she spoke out loud

In the manner of partners who have spent a great deal of their life together - Damian had followed her train of thought as her expressions changed on her face, even though she hadn't verbalised anything up to that point.

Remember that quote from John and Lyn St Clair Thomas…

"For those who believe, no proof is necessary, for those who don't believe no proof is possible

That's fine for spirituality, Marietta replied - but what we're talking about is most definitely about the body, not the spirit.

Damian nodded at this, but not in agreement

"yes it's true our solution is about the body, but where would the spirit be without a vessel - and we don't have much time"

Now it was Marisa's turn to agree - "time is running out, no doubt"

**Blue Mountains, Australia**

**February 3rd, 2023**

Marietta tapped away on her keyboard, as Damian suggested ideas for the final section of the proposal.

As she hit the enter key for the last time, she said - 'well that's it - either they think we're completely crazy or they give us a chance' - either way - it's done!

Right, let's get Alfred to sort out the translations and get it off via secure FTP transfer this evening to the committee.

"Ok, but first I need a walk - lets get changed and walk the National Pass - I need some air" Marisa replied.

They put on their bushwalking gear and headed out into the warm evening - it was just past 6pm, but it wouldn't get dark here in the Southern Hemisphere until close to 9pm.

They had plenty of time to do the walk, which started with a steep descent down old metal stairs to a walkway halfway down the escarpment of the spectacular Blue Mountains on the western edge and 100 kilometres from the centre of Australia's harbourside city.

The National Pass was their favourite walk - a 4.5km loop that featured spectacular views down the valley, and of the nearby waterfall plunging into the Jamison Valley.

To their south, was to all intents and purposes a complete wilderness, with only scattered old ghost towns - it really was a place where humans were not at home. A eucalypt, fern and pine dominated national park where not too long before a relic population of Wollemi Pine - a tree only known from the Fossil Record - had been discovered by bush walkers who then informed local scientists.

The Wollemi was a part of a plant family going back more than 200 million years, and less than 100 adult trees survived in the wild. Although it was now a common and popular garden plant, grown by many enthusiastic supporters of one of the world's most spectacular conservation successes.

But the Wollemi was further west and to the north. The trees of the National Pass, no less spectacular but much less rare - Sydney Blue Gum, Paperbarks, Yellow Pittosporum, Bracken Ferns and more.

As they hiked along, they discussed the proposal they had just completed - as if they were in a high school debate team - Damian taking the negative argument and pushing Marietta so that she was prepared for what came next.

A presentation to a UN emergency council meeting - provided the committee agreed with their proposal in principle it would then have to be ratified by the full UN emergency council before being given funding by the Global Rescue Fund(The GRF) that had been established by all member countries.

The GRF was exploring and funding all sorts of programs, from alternative food sources, to establishing a colony on the moon and Mars using Falcon Heavy Rockets from Elon Musk's Space X company.

It was looking at building underground food production units - secured bunkers using hydroponics and aeroponics, protected by impressive military bases.

It was funding research into stasis pods straight out of Star Trek.

In more esoteric research, it was funding a revisiting of spirituality mind control techniques from tribal cultures as old as the Australian

Aboriginals to the Red Indian tribes and East Asian mystics - aiming to see if there was a way humans could operate on less food than they usually required to live.

Anything and everything was being explored in this last ditch effort to save the human species from complete destruction.

Surely Marietta argued that if mystics could get a hearing, then hard science with credentialed scientists would be given a go.

Mmmm, Damian answered - yes but mind control is one thing - messing with our genes is another! - even the church considers genes the gift from god, and it's not up to us to mess with them on this scale.

"Even if we cease to exist?" She said!

"Yep, exactly. But that isn't going to stop us is it?" he said, encouraging her as he always did.

"Not if I have anything to do with it, she answered"

**CSIRO Presentation to the UN Global Fund**

**Geneva**
**7th March, 2023**

Damian walked to the lectern, carrying a single sheet of A5 paper. He adjusted the microphone and clicked a single slide up on the massive screen in the UN conference hall.

He looked out across the 167 delegates - ambassadors from every member country of the UN.

Thank you to the delegates of this emergency UN Global Fund Summit - as you all know only too well, we are less than 3 years away from a complete breakdown of the global food production engine.

A massive destruction of the global bee population, combined with increasing global temperatures and the disaster of the Cynata GMO cropping release have combined in a perfect storm.

Despite the short term solution delivered by my research colleague - Marietta - we are now facing catastrophe that will make nuclear war look like the Mad Hatter's tea party.

We have been invited to present to you a bold plan, one which would have seemed crazy just a few years ago.

It's one that we believe has a chance of saving at least half of the world's population.

Without it, we'll be back to the stone age within 5 years. A small few tribes of the remaining humans on the planet may survive, but it will be a thousand years before the human race numbers in the billions again.

Whilst I have worked on the team that devised this protocol, it is led of course by my wife - Nobel Prize for Chemistry winner - Professor Marietta de Pietra.

Please welcome her to the stage to present the proposal to you.

Damian stepped off the stage, briefly holding his wife's hand and giving her a quick kiss on the cheek as she stepped up the 3 short stairs onto the stage.

Marietta looked apprehensive - she wasn't a natural presenter - and was better discussing ideas in small groups.

But at this moment, a certainty and composure lifted her delivery in a presentation that would go down in history to rival those speeches of Martin Luther King - "I have a dream" and John F Kennedy's speech on landing men on the moon.

For 30 minutes she detailed the experiment they had devised including the hoped for outcome that would once and for all save, yet change the entire human race.

Bold was an understatement.

For years, the global human population had put a ban on genetic modification of human beings directly. Cloning was banned. Sure, some genetic disease modification had been allowed, such as in utero insertion of gene modifiers that had helped cure heart conditions, and certain other diseases like diabetes.

But outright changing of the basic human genome was beyond the pale - at least until the entire survival of the human race was on the table.

Marietta explained how the insertion of a small genetically modified algae, carried in a viral transport matrix would be injected under the skin of first non primates, then primates and finally humans on an accelerated 6 month project.

The concept was to bioform the human race to be able to produce its own food via photosynthesis - the process by which green plants use sunlight to synthesize nutrients from carbon dioxide and water using the pigment chlorophyll.

There was a double benefit to this project - it would not only allow humans to produce nutrients, but also would produce oxygen as well - with the rise in the carbon dioxide levels on the planet due to the collapse of higher order agriculture plants, humans would replace their food with own made, and produce oxygen to breathe too.

At first shocked, and despite a thirty minute uproar caused by the leaders of several religion first countries - gradually Marietta won the delegates over with her candour and genius - showing them that there really was no other way left for the human race to go - food production was collapsing, corn, oats, wheat were dying all over the planet due to corporate greed and mono species exposure.

And the substrate required for her Nobel prize winning food production units was running out too.

In the end, the delegates voted by an overwhelming majority of 150 to 17 to approve the funding required for Marietta and her team to conduct the research.

Sydney was again chosen mainly due to the success of their teams work on the food production unit and that fact the lab was up and running and secure.

The ease of quarantining the Island Continent of Australia was also a key factor in the second solution - the irony of which was not lost on this nation that commenced its history with invasion and servitude started by convicts and colonists.

As an island continent, Australia had had millions of years of isolation from the rest of the world, and so had developed its own animal and plant species unique on the planet - kangaroos, koalas, echidna, platypus were well known.

Not so well known were the millions of plants and invertebrates that made up a wholly unique biota of this Southern Hemisphere Continent - the largest of all islands.

The concept also wasn't lost on the first peoples of Australia who had developed the world's oldest surviving culture of over 60000 years due to the isolation of the Australian continent.

The members of the UN security council insisted that scientists from key European, Asian, African and American countries were represented on the research team - to which Marietta and Damian heartily agreed as long as they were able to select the right mix of skills and experience across those member countries.

# North Head Quarantine Station

## June 2023

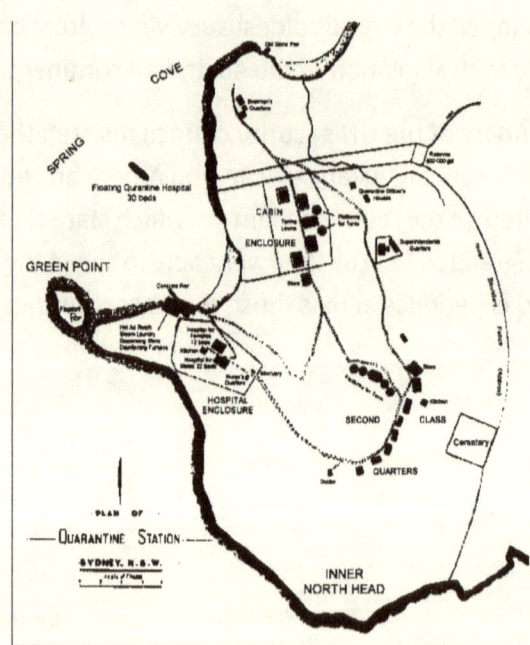

"What about Professor MacKenzie from Scotland" said Giacomo?

"Oh god no" Damian said, "he's a drunk, tells awful jokes over and over, and he always smells like a cross between an old spice ad and a distillery"

"But he is brilliant with viral transport" Giacomo countered, and are we going to let a bad sense of humour and a little scotch get in the way?"

"Yep, we need to get this job done quick, and we can't have any interruptions from an old soak, let's move on"

Giacomo put the folder down, and started flicking through a big pile of orange folders with confidential stamped across them. A much smaller pile sat next to it on the table demonstrating to them all how little progress they had made in the last 48 hours.

"I need a coffee" Giacomo Announced and got up and slouched over to the coffee machine in the commissary.

"He's right you know" Marisa said, as she watched him move away.

"We need to finalise the rest of the team quickly, it isn't easy, and perhaps a few foibles will have to be overlooked"

"What I didn't say is he also can't keep his hands off the ladies, so I don't think so" Damian said with some finality, and a little smirk.

"Someone has to watch out for you" he added.

"Well thanks for the gallantry, and ok, we'll move on"

"Dr Peters from Boston looks like a good alternative, she published that excellent paper on germ cell gene therapy last year"

"Ok, here's Giacomo - hey what about Dr Peters mate?" Damian quizzed his colleague and best friend"

"Yes, now we're talking, she knows her stuff, and doesn't smell like whisky which is good" Giacomo said, laughing - "sorry guys, I'm just feeling a little ragged from setting up the lab and trying to do a recruitment job in 48 hours that would normally take months"

"We understand" Marietta and Damian chorussed.

"Snap" said Marietta, and they all laughed in unison.

"Well my eyes are hanging out of my head - I vote we take an hour, get some food and take a quick walk down to Shelley Beach and get the guards to pick us up at the bottom of the hill.

It will clear our heads to get out in the sun for a bit, and I'm sure we'll be able to finish the team selection much quicker" Marietta suggested.

"I'm in" Damian said.

"Ok, If I have to" Giacomo said - but secretly he was happy to get the hell out of this 1930's building with the crappy old vinyl floor tiles that dated from before the second world war.

He was happy in a modern lab, but was famously snobbish about old buildings after having to spend most of his first years in a clapped out lab come workshop in an old CSIRO building in Castle Hill after he graduated.

They all got up and headed over to the kitchen server area to see what was on for food - hoping it wasn't boiled chicken and vegetables again.

Marietta made a mental note to chat to the base captain and see if they couldn't get a better menu sorted before the international scientists arrived.

There'd be no pleasing the Europeans and the Asians with that offering, although then she caught herself and thought they really should be happy with anything, given most of the world was existing on algiprote from her food production machines.

In the end she realised, it was a good thing the base had its own vegetable garden and chickens, but it wouldn't feed a hundred hungry scientists working on a round the clock schedule starting the following month.

After eating some dinner, the three headed off from the top of the North Head Park, down to the Q Station and then across the huge parade ground and onto the metal walkways at the start of the heads to beach walk.

It was a short 2.7 kilometre walk, and mostly downhill but enough to invigorate them and get their heads clearer.

After the walk, they got on the radio and called the guard station to pick them up just around from Shelly Beach.

A guard turned up in a Bushmaster Truck - manufactured and produced in Australia for the Australian armed forces.

The demise of commercial vehicle production in Australia in the mid teens made the Bushmaster the only locally produced Australian vehicle.

The guard drove them back up to the base where they continued the team selection - finally concluding the task around 9.30pm.

"Ok that's it then, are we all done" Marietta asked.

"I'm happy said Giacomo, I can work with all my team and if any are unavailable then the two alternates are fine too"

"Ha!" Damian laughed. "If anyone thinks they will have a fair excuse for not turning up when called, I'll be keen to hear it"

He laughed again and added "Anyway, I'm done too, I'm confident we can work a solution with this team"

"Ok then" Marietta stood up and stretched - "I'll get on to sending an email to Angelique to square it away.

"Then I'm going to turn in and get an early one - we have a lot to do to prepare for their arrival"

"See you shortly" Damian said as she left.

"How about a quick game of table tennis?", Damian said as he also stood up and stretched - popping the ligaments in his shoulders as he crossed his arms over his chest

"Oh god, you'll kill me, but yes all right" Giacomo said.

They walked over to the table tennis table on the other side of the commissary, and proceeded to relive their university college rivalry for a few minutes before heading to bed. It was a chance to just enjoy a little friendly competition and stop thinking about the enormity of the challenge that faced them.

Picking a few brilliant scientists from a table full of folders of brilliant scientists was one thing.

Actually getting this idea to work was quite another.

"We're actually doing this, aren't we" Giacomo said after smashing a high bouncing ball which nicked the edge of Damian's end of the table. "And that's 19 to you and 1 to me he laughed after finally getting his first point.

"Yep, seems that way" Damian said in an understated ironic way.

"The first approved trials in human bioforming, oh dear I hope we're doing the right thing" Giacomo commented.

"I'm not sure either" said Damian. "But what choice do we have?, all the other ideas were explored when we came up with the Food Production Unit"

"And if anyone is going to do this seemingly crazy thing, and make it work, I'm happy to be in the centre of it, because at least we can have some control over the outcome and use of this technology and genetics"

"Yeah, imagine if you know who got a hold of it"

"Yeah, the nameless ones"

"There'd be people disappearing off the street and who knows what they'd try - instead of food requirements, they'd be developing walking, talking bioweapons" opined Giacomo.

"Yeah, imagine"

"Yeah..."

In their typical laconic Australian manner, the two men continued the game, both still torn between the goals of saving the human race with bio forming and destroying it with the same technology.

Despite being scientists who were about to do what many called playing God, they were at heart good people who were just trying the best with the knowledge and skills they possessed.

The desire to help others was a constant in social people all over the planet - a key part of the definition of what it meant to be human.

Of course there was a small percentage of people on the Earth who were the very embodiment of evil, and some of these ran the nameless countries that the boys spoke of with an iron fist, and only greed in their hearts.

So yes, indeed whilst Marietta, Damian, Giacomo and the rest of the scientists who had been chosen were chosen on their scientific expertise, they were all also chosen because they were trying to do good. There was no personal benefit to their work, only a philanthropic aspiration.

This didn't mean it would all turn out well for them or anyone for that matter, but for that only time would tell.

# North Head Quarantine Station
# Manly
# September, 2023

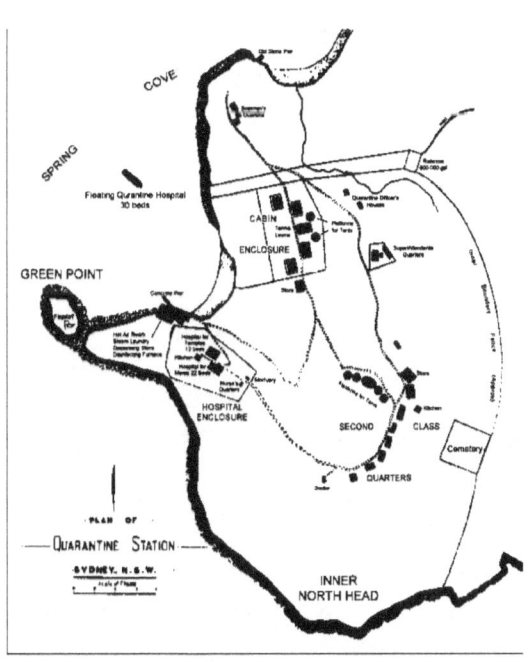

"Don't you think it's kind of ironic that they chose our lab and Australia as the location for this project - quarantined by thousands of kilometres of ocean all around?" - Giacomo mused to Damian as they walked up the covered walkway towards the common room to get ready for the new arrivals.

"I find it more ironic that we're operating in what used to be a quarantine station for new arrivals to Australia, in the middle of bushland on the edge of Australia's largest city. "We're working in a biohazard quarantine lab, quarantined in a quarantine station, within a 5 kilometre quarantine zone, on a quarantined island - it's enough levels to do your head in"

"I used to walk here on the weekends during University - and when I was really feeling fit, I'd start at the Spit, walk to Manly for lunch, and then continue on up the hill and do the circuit through the quarantine station too"

"Standing in that parade ground is positively eerie late in the evening when everyone else has gone home"

"Well it's hardly eerie now with helicopters landing every few minutes to ferry in scientists and supplies"

As if on cue, a US Army Black Hawk blew over their heads and cycled down onto the parade ground right behind their building.

That will be the Yanks now - sped here, courtesy of the Pacific 7th Fleet.

"With the airports all closed, it was the only way they could get here inside of a month." Damian noted.

Giacomo rolled his eyes, thinking about how noisy it was about to get around here with the Americans in town.

Dr Peter Curtis from the University of Alabama was a fine scientist, but he was as annoying as they came in conversation - always wanting the last word, and speaking about 30 decibels louder than anyone else as he pontificated on his algal research work in the bayou.

Oh well, he sighed as he turned and moved away with Damian - we'd better go and play host… but god help us.

At 9.30pm that night, the base commander called a meeting of all personnel. Brigadier Steven Perkins was a 6 foot 3 inch mountain of a bloke who had grown up in country NSW before joining the army twenty years before.

Even though he was now in his late 50's, he still had a ramrod straight back, and the bearing of a man who was confident yet not arrogant. His iron fist in a velvet glove approach to leading his men in war time and peace was renowned throughout the Australian armed forces.

In his decorated military career, he had served in various locations around the world - although the exact nature of his service was classified as he was originally a member of the renowned Australian S.A.S or Special Air Service.

After an operational incident and receiving wounds that included pieces of shrapnel lodged close to his spine he was taken off active special forces duty. He was awarded command of various units back in Australia and he was an obvious choice for this specific posting. His job was protecting a group of scientists who were the last best hope for human kind. He was tough in keeping the base protection disciplined, but he was also an excellent communicator who listened and made things happen. He understood people well.

"Listen up everyone" and within seconds you could hear a pin drop - there was no continued murmuring of conversation dying away slowly like you'd expect in a room full of people. It was absolute immediate silence.

"I'm going to turn you over to Dr Costa shortly, but before I do I want to cover a few simple rules for your time here at the base"

"Before I go over those, I have to inform you that as of now, the base is on permanent lockdown. The UN has had a leak of the information about the trial and the base location. It means we're going to have plenty of individuals and groups wanting to disrupt what you're doing. And they now know where you are"

"There was a collective groan from the group, who understand that was it for them enjoying any down time in the beautiful heathland bush and surrounds of the base"

"Ok I understand, but that's how it going to have to be if I have any chance of keeping you protected"

"One - obviously now, don't leave the base without informing someone of where you need to go - we'll then provide an escort after determining if it's safe to do so."

"Please don't be outside at night after 11pm - the eyes of the world are going to be on this place and we can't guarantee your safety at night with the bush so close around us. We'll have patrols, movement senses, and teams out in the bush, but this is a big property and there are no fences."

"If there is an alert, you'll hear a klaxon horn, like this" - he motioned to his lieutenant commander who pressed a button on a walkie talkie, said something into it and seconds later there was a loud whooping sound like full time at the footy.

"when you do, assemble here in the commissary immediately, and we'll escort you to the shelters - drop everything, I don't care if you're in the middle of an experiment - it means immediate danger to the base"

"if you have a problem with accomodations or food, see Lieutenant Peters here"

"if you have a problem with scientific equipment or supplies see Professor Di Tano"

Thank you for your attention, and here's Professor Marietta Costa.

As Marietta walked over to the lectern there was spontaneous applause from everyone in the room - an acknowledgement from her professional peers at her achievements with the Nobel Prize

Marietta smiled , and accepted the acknowledgement with grace and after a few moments held out her arms and acknowledged all the other members of her team standing to her left and then moved her arms to the front and with palms turned down and motioned for them to finish.

"Thank you" she said.

"I appreciate your acknowledgement, but from this moment forward I am just one of the team. I'm here to participate, and also to help you get what you need from the UN, so I don't want you putting me on any sort of a pedestal please, ok?"

"Yes!" almost everyone in the room chorussed.

"Ok, then let's get on with it" Marietta said with the exact right amount of force.

"You all know what you're here for and what we have to try and do - you've all received briefing documents"

"All the botanists can now go with Damian to start work on the algae identification, selection and culturing" - about 20 people moved off with Damian and left the room.

"All the geneticists - you're with Giacomo to work on the germ cell replication issues - a small group of 8 left with Giacomo.

"The intensivists and nursing staff, can you go start setting up for the experiments and clinical studies in the secure base hospital ward - and don't forget your swipe cards. A dozen or so left the room and headed for the hospital building.

"All the virologists are with me, we're going to focus on the viral transport issues" - she led a group of about 16 people out of the room leaving only the military personnel.

Brigadier Perkins said.

"And you lot, get back to post and keep me in the loop if anyone ignores the rules"

"Sir, Yes Sir" - the dozen or so soldiers snapped a salute and hurried from the room.

Brigadier Perkins went over to the coffee machine and made himself a coffee - black, no sugar. Simple and no nonsense just like himself.

He grabbed a ham and cheese sandwich from the commissary fridge and sat down by the window looking over the parade ground.

He ate the sandwich in silence, and drank the coffee in one gulp. He was obviously mulling over private thoughts as he sat there looking into the middle distance focussed on nothing in particular.

To no one in particular he said 'ok, well let's see what these scientists have got". It was said in a respectful yet hopeful manner that they indeed could solve the problem.

Yes without a solution, the human race was in severe trouble - and as a career military man that meant he had a job to do. But as a father of three children, he was also thinking that a successful result was more important to his kids and the next generation around the world than him.

He nodded to himself 'ok, lets see" and he stood up and marched out of the room as only a military man can do.

## Two Weeks Later

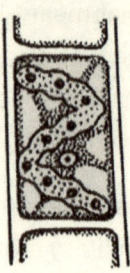

It had been a gruelling couple of weeks. With the intensity that always came at the start of any group project, all the teams had thrown themselves at their respective tasks.

All had been operating on too little sleep and Marietta had eventually had to institute a lab curfew to ensure people got some shut eye.

Even then individual scientists and small groups sat up in their lodgings - too wired to sleep - discussing and arguing hypotheses and ideas and results well into the early hours most nights.

The upside was they made some good progress, the downside was people were starting to make mistakes, and they were getting agitated with each other.

After a few nasty spats in the dining hall, Marietta turned to the Brigadier Perkins who helped her solve it.

"You have to tire them out physically" he said - "their minds are racing a million miles and hour, but they are not getting any exercise"

And so the entire base was turned out that evening for a literal military boot camp in the parade ground - one of the Brigadiers sergeants took them through 45 minutes of calisthenics, and running including wind sprints, burpees and more.

Of course, few of the scientists were used to exercising so much, other than Marietta and Damian who walked a lot - but even they felt the pain in their muscles by the end.

Over the next couple of months, Giacomo injected a little fun and humour as he always did - he mixed project teams into groups and came up with some statistics and goals with the winning team having the best combined physical statistics improvement - weight, heart rate, muscle strength and so forth.

It worked a dream, everyone started sleeping well at night, falling into their beds exhausted each evening.

They also all got fitter, and more productive at their work as well, so even though they weren't putting in as many hours, they actually got more done.

The first breakthrough was with the delivery system - an innovative hypospray device based on an idea that the Scottish scientist - Kennedy - had seen on Star Trek of all things.

They celebrated that evening by switching the board tracking to green on that project, and hosting a showing of an original star trek episode featuring James T Kirk and Dr McCoy saving a previously unknown lifeform.

They also watched the original Triffids movie on TV, featuring a plant that is transformed to be able to move and then begins preying on humans.

That was Giacomo's dark sense of humour at play again.

It was all going brilliantly well, until the Klaxon Horn went off one morning at 3am.

The horn was piercing and continued blasting through the base until every scientist was accounted for and in the shelters.

As the last of them moved down the stairs into the old bunker, they heard a deep booming sound and then felt rather than heard a vibration through their bodies and feet.

That hurried everyone up, and the door was shut behind them - lights flickering to life in the bunker like a scene from the blitz in a World War Two movie.

The bunker was huge and well appointed, so they would be both safe and comfortable down here, but it didn't assuage the concern they had about the noise and vibration they had heard as they entered the bunker.

"What was that? a scientist finally said out loud"

Just as he finished asking the question, the door opened and the Brigadier walked in. He was looking sharp and alert as you'd expect, not like he had just been roused from his bed just a few minutes previously.

Unlike the scientists who were in a range of sleeping wear, or covered in blankets, he was in full operational uniform - dark green pants, t-shirt, vest and black boots.

He said "ok, thanks everyone for following my instructions - first up - everything is fine"

"There was an improvised fertiliser bomb detonated down at the bottom of the hill, outside the front gates.

"It was only small, and meant as a diversion for a small group of protesters coming up the path from Shelly Beach" he added.

"But we caught them, they're from a small fringe group who are against bio forming and whilst they used a bomb, they actually had no weapons - only spray cans and loud hailers"

"Apparently they were intent on just causing disruption and voicing their opposition"

He then went on to explain that just to be safe, they would stay here until morning and until all the patrols had reported in.

Everything passed uneventfully for that evening, the next day, and most of the next month.

In the meantime, the team also discovered several strong candidates for the algae they would use, and testing started on each of these including sensitivity tests on the skin of rabbits and monkeys, the ability to scale up colonies of the algae to the quantities that would be required for global dosing.

The final scaling to full quantities would be done in the massive algae production factories used for the first food production unit - they were basically large ponds situated near the worlds oceans in New Zealand, Tasmania, Hawaii, Mexico and Southern Africa.

These had been co-opted by the UN for this project.

But the science team still had to prove the science, maths and growth rates in order to provide calculations for the factories to follow to prepare the 'vaccination' which had been nicknamed Genetech P.S. (The P.S. was short for Photosynthesis and also Para Skin or 'by the skin')


More serious than the protesters and then improvised bomb, was the discovery that one of the Chinese Scientists was spying on the project.

It was a chance comment by one of the listening post military personnel one evening that led to their discovery.

Brigadier Perkins was standing behind the radio operators in the previously secret base below the Quarantine Reserve.

"Anything to report Airman?"

"Sir, not much going on, Sir" Airman Ho replied.

"We have a Wallenius Wilhelmsen container ship passing through the heads under the direction of the Harbour Pilot, a US refuelling barge also heading out to the 7th Fleet off shore, and a yacht with a broken mast waiting for a tow back into the harbour"

"Ok, thanks Airman, anything else?"

The Brigadier knew from long experience that sometimes the first report wasn't all the report, but junior officers often felt they didn't want to waste the time of senior officers, and so would shorten reports to a few key elements in response.

"Sir?" The Airman enquired?

"I'm interested in anything on any frequency within 10 kilometres of this base" The Brigadier replied.

He knew of course that the listening post was tracking every frequency using powerful signal tracking software. Keywords and sentence structure were programmed into the system and using scanning and recording facilities were checked over carefully to find any anomalies.

"Well Sir, there is one thing" Airman Ho added.

"Yes?"

"Well Sir, there have been a couple of kids chatting in a MIN dialect on a CB radio tonight, and I only mention it because they seem to be on air about the same time each week"

"Min?" Perkins said

Airman Ho was 2nd generation Australian, and identified as an Aussie with as broad an accent as you'd expect from any young Australian kid.

But his father's mother - his grandma - had come from Fujian province in China where the Min language was spoken by just a few ten's of millions of people.

It was virtually unknown outside China - where Mandarin(the official language of China) and Cantonese were the ones that had achieved recognition in the west and which were taught in schools and featured in movies and books.

"Sir, it's a dialect language from China - my grandmother spoke it, and taught me when I was younger"

Of course many of the listening post staff were multilingual and interested in languages - it was one of the things that ensured their recruitment in this division of the armed forces - much like the 'wind talkers' of the Indian nations were used for coded transmissions in the second world war with American forces.

"What are they talking about?" Brigadier Perkins asked.

"It seems to be a conversation about school, and their music lessons" Airman Ho replied.

"But I'm unsure as to why they would be using CB radio channels and the signals are quite weak - they'd only go a kilometre or so, and we're only picking them up because they are bouncing off the sandstone cliffs around here and hitting our sensitive receiving dishes"

"So what's the issue Airman?" Perkins persisted, seeing that the Airman was puzzling over something.

"Sir, it's just that Min is not an official language, and the children seem quite young, and well…" he hesitated before being prompted to go on.

"Well Sir, I can't be sure, but the signal seems to be originating from the middle of the Dobroyd Head, on the Spit to Manly walk"

"I'm sure it's just the signal bouncing around, it's probably further up the hill in Balgowlah Heights." he finished and continued to look mildly perplexed.

"Well Airman, we're not going to make an assumption are we" Perkins said

"Sir, no sir" Airman Ho replied, suitably chastened at this reminder of the listening posts motto - "nulla principia falsi" - which literally meant no assumptions.

It had been coined by the original listening post personnel on the day it was officially inaugurated in the 1960's.

And was meant to remind all personnel that listening was one thing, deciphering and understanding was another.

Sound waves could be used to transmit any message - coded or uncoded - and sometimes one was assumed to be the other.

Perkins immediately dispatched a squad under the command of Sergeant Annabelle Peters. She was a bush craft specialist and knew the local bushland better than most, having grown up in nearby Balgowlah. Peters had competed in multiple cross country events, and prior to joined the reserves and then the regular army had been a school and university champion.

Her uncle, also a keen bushwalker, had been part of the group who had fought the government to protect the Crater Cove cabins on the harbour below Dobroyd Head.

Co-incidentally, that was where they found a cache of food, camping gear, and a walkie talkie with spare batteries.

They staked out the cabins for close to a week, before catching one of the base scientists, who had been sneaking out of the quarantine station and making the 6.2 kilometre trek along the Manly to Spit walk and down to the Crater Cove cabins to transmit her weekly report to a fishing boat moored offshore near Lady Bay beach.

The fishing boat was then heading out to sea each week and transferring the data to a Chinese naval ship in international waters.

Whilst the transmission picked up by Airman Ho sounded like a couple of young kids chatting away, it was just the high pitch of the scientists voice and that of the individual she was speaking to on the fishing boat.

The Chinese government had a long history of spying on both commercial and government operations around the world. The operational basis of most Chinese organisations including the military was to copy others technology rather than innovate.

They had been banned from being part of 5G mobile networks because of their influence over the company Huawei in the 2010's.

All Chinese Scientists on the team were dismissed from the project team and alternates were brought in.

The Chinese Government lodged an official complaint with the UN, but they were given short shrift on that when the details of their spying were released directly to the world's media.

The incident threw the whole team into a fugue for a couple of weeks - they had liked the Chinese Scientist and she had contributed a lot to the project - and to find out she was a spy was a shock for many of them.

Finally they got back into the full swing of the project.

And the next milestone was significant, not just for the project, but for the entire history of genetic modification science.

Giacomo stood up in front of the group. They were all gathered in the largest of the labs on the base for a demonstration.


"Ok, so you can see here on the big screen a high powered microscopic image of a cell - in this case it's a single cell that we've exposed to the adenovirus vector" Damian began his explanation.

Giacomo's team were exploring both somatic gene therapy - where modified genetic material is inserted into a tissue of the patients body, and germ line therapy where the modified genetic material would be introduced into reproductive cells.

Although the study at this stage had only been approved for somatic therapy in adults - they knew it would only be a matter of time before they had to explore the germ line therapy to for the next generation of children to survive in a world without traditional food production.

Giacomo continued with his explanation.

"The problem we were having with the adenovirus is that it was successfully attaching to mid level skin cells, but they were immediately rejecting the algal DNA fragment"

The physical manifestation of this was that layers of skin on the test subjects was dying and peeling off within days of the injections.

"We explored the human genetic blueprint for some evidence of how mitochondria were introduced into cells without rejection"

It was thought by scientists that mitochondria - the little 'batteries' of animal cells had actually started life as a separate single cell organism and at some point in history had been incorporated into the cells of early animals and lost their individuality.

"Mitochondria were 'assimilated' much like the Borg assimilate species in Star Trek" Damian added, which got a chuckle from a few of the American and Australian Scientists.

The joke was lost on Scientists from those countries where Star Trek wasn't as popular, yet Damian pushed the analogy a little further.

"Our cells, or should I say the cells of our ancient forebears some six hundred million years ago, captured or entered a symbiotic relationship with Mitochondria"

"Mitochondria - as many of you know - have their own distinct independent genome that shows similarity with bacteria, and this is where this hypothesis originated"

"Anyway, the great news is, we've worked out how to get the virus to transfer our modified genetic material to the Mitochondria instead"

The room erupted in cheers and whoops from the scientists who knew this breakthrough was huge.

When the applause died down - Giacomo acknowledged one of his team

"Without a little inspiration from Dr Chiogi from Kyoto, we'd never have made this leap"

"The room turned it's collective attention to the diminutive Japanese geneticist, who had triggered the work towards this incredible breakthrough"

Taking a laser pointer from Giacomo, Dr Chiogi said his thanks to the group, and proceeded to explain the details of the breakthrough.

"Shielded by a "known" component of the cell, the mitochondria can then be switched on to replicate and grow the photosynthetic material within their mini compound in the cell"

"It all ends up the same - we get a cell that actually can then engage in photosynthesis without the rejection and death of the skin cell"

"It also encapsulates the material and stops it being transferred deeper into the tissue or via the blood - since Red Blood Cells have no mitochondria"

It actually was the last barrier to the project, since without it, they would never have been able to move forward with phase III experiments - the introduction of the actually gene load into animal skin to see what happened.

And now they could begin the next step.

"One last thing" - Giacomo said - "can we have a green please"

And with a flourish he gestured to the large computer screen that had become their guidon over the past few months.

The final red light next to the genetics team project list switched over to green and the room again erupted in applause.

"I think we deserve a short break" said Marietta and the group immediately headed for the commissary to toast their celebration with non-alcoholic grape juice"

As they left, Marietta took Giacomo aside with Dr Chiogi

"Very well done" she said.

"Thanks boss" Damian said smiling a cheesy grin.

"Arigatou gozaimasu Marietta san" added Dr Ciogi with a deep bow to Marietta.

Marietta returned a even deeper, respectful bow to Dr Chiogi saying at the same time "you have given us a chance Dr Chiogi, and we thank you for your professional and dedicated contribution"

As she finished this acknowledgement, she held out one hand and gestured for them both to accompany her to join the team.

As they walked off, she enquired of Dr Chiogi

"Perhaps you will celebrate by playing some music Akihito"

"Only if you will accompany me on the Taiko drum" replied Chiogi.

"Haha" replied Marietta, "if only I had any sense of rhythm, perhaps you can recruit Giacomo here into your entourage, I'd only put your timing off"

They both laughed and headed off to the commissary.

Dr Chiogi made a detour and grabbed his Shamisen - a three stringed banjo like Japanese instrument popular in theatre and folk music.

Dr Chiogi was well known in scientific circles for his musical ability which paralleled his scientific credentials.

Whilst the music didn't follow the same familiar musical structure of western music, the group nonetheless enjoyed his music for an hour or so, whilst they took a well earned break from the intense lab work.

Whilst they were officially taking a break, much of the smaller group conversations over refreshments were about the breakthrough and what this meant for the overall project, it really was a major milestone and a move into a new phase of the project.

Now the fundamentals were in place, they could begin the clinical work - to see if their pre-clinical lab work on the dosing, transport and genetics would actually work in allowing them to bio form a living organism.

**CSIRO Human Bioforming Lab**

**North Head Quarantine Station**

**Sydney Australia**

**August 2024**

What do you mean you've injected yourself? interrupted Damian.

"Are you insane.." added Marietta as they both shook their heads in unison at Giacomo's revelation.

"We haven't got time to waste, there are hundreds of thousands of people dying every day we wait, and the damn ethics committee is still sitting on their arses about it." Giacomo said, responding with an equally forceful answer.

Giacomo had always been the fiery member of the team, even in university days, he had often stretched the rules at the University lab to breaking point - his brilliance the only thing that saved him from being expelled during his PhD year.

"Anyway, we're only going to find out if this works one way. And that's test it on a live subject."

"But what about the blood factors" Marietta enjoined.

"You know you're not the best match for the experiment - your white cells are highly sensitive, even more so than normal with your childhood leukaemia. We've no idea if they'll attack the viral transport or not. Even though it's been masked and engineered to ensure it only stays in the capillaries close to the skin. It can't survive closer to the body core"

Well, I took the hypospray doser 30 minutes ago, so we'll find out fairly soon - I estimate within the next 10 mins.

All three looked over at the clock on the wall as the red second hand sped around to the 12 position, and then started another circuit around the dial.

"Right, get the ice vest on now to protect your core from overheating, and turn out the lights and we'll see what's going on" - Damian said

As soon as Damian hit the lights, they could immediately see the initial effects of the dosing on Giacomo's skin.

It was already slightly luminescent. Especially on his left arm near the site of the injection. It was already spreading in little green highways along this arms and across his neck.

Giacomo was bare chested except for the ice vest.

Damian asked him to roll up the base of his pants and they saw the luminescent tinge already starting on his legs too.

OK, hit the UV lights.

Even more dramatic, they could see the coloration under UV and the hub points up and down his arms - these would become structures very much like the small stomata on plants where the sugars production would be controlled all over Giacomo's body - the heart of the chlorophyll pump network.

If this worked, he'd soon be starting to produce his own food from the residual water and nutrients in his body.

They had seen temperature spikes in some of the early animal experiments and had found that ice vests helped keep the bodies cool during the early parts of the experiment.

Damian said - ok, physically it looks good, but I want you to lie down and plug in the vitals so we can start the monitoring immediately and just in case your blood pressure drops from the infection or your insulin kicks in too hard with the sugars.

Giacomo lay down on the gurney in the lab and dutifully attached a heart rate monitor patches to his chest and a finger tip pulse monitor as well.

In the meantime, Damian called the base Intensivist and got them started on checking Damian out. They would draw blood, check his vitals, and complete a myriad of other tests.

Giacomo would have to get used to the pushing and prodding and the tests which would become routine every hour for the rest of that day, whilst they determined the effects of the injections.

Marietta said, "I'll have to inform Angelique so she can tell the UN ethics committee - they're not going to be happy. I'll be back"

And with that she swept out of the lab and headed to the office areas to call the Chairman - a call she was dreading - although Giacomo may just win a medal for his crazy stupid actions.

If it worked he could be a saviour to tens of millions, by bringing forward the project by weeks.

Whilst they all cared deeply about the project they were working on, all 50 plus scientists from around the globe - Giacomo was as always putting everything into it - including in this case potentially putting his life on the line.

**UN Compound**

**Offices of the Ethics Committee Chair**

**New York**

**August 2024**

The phone buzzed insistently as the Ethics Chairwoman - Angelique Charpentier walked into her office after another gruelling committee meeting to talk about the Human Bioforming project being run in Sydney.

Angelique had been listening to her committee all day, and they were no nearer making a decision on the proposal from Marietta and Damian.

Angelique had the utmost respect for her two colleagues on the other side of the world, and she was inclined to come down on the affirmative side and let the experiment go ahead. After all, risking a few lives to save millions, perhaps billions seemed sensible to her.

But some of her colleagues were stuck in the methodology of all ethics committees from the past, and not willing to move from their position that every life was sacred and the drug trial phases would have to be completed in order - albeit at a castle accelerated rate.

But by then, they were staring down the barrel of a 50% reduction in the global population - it couldn't be worse, and the UN in their wisdom had appointed her as the final arbiter - not politicians, not UN officials, not corporations, not the heads of Churches - she!

Mon dieu - her head was spinning.

She grabbed the headset and plonked down into the reading chair near the window. Feeling drained to the point of near exhaustion.

Allo? She said in a musical tone.

And within seconds the look of exhaustion was replaced with incredulity at the words she heard from Marietta calling from Sydney.

"What! Are you joking?"

"mmm hmmm"

"mmm hmmm"

Angelique listened and nodded her head a couple of times as Marietta filled her in.

She then acknowledged her, ended the call, and ran out of the office.

Her next stop the office of the Secretary General.

As she left the office, she yelled out to her secretary to keep the ethics committee in the conference room, and tell them she would be with them in 5 minutes.

# Quarantine Station

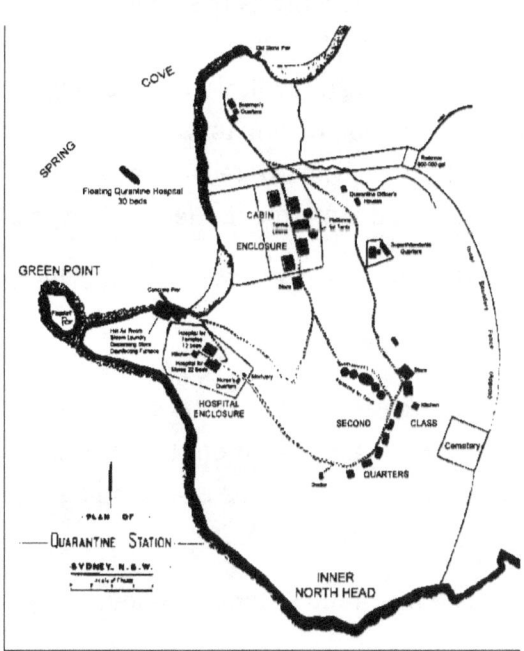

As it turned out, their initial fears were unfounded. Giacomo was stable for the next three weeks.

After the tests showed he was doing well, the doctors allowed him to be mobilised in a wheel chair. He had to drag around some fluids, but the rest of the monitoring was being done by a series of small patch devices that Giacomo either stuck on his skin, or licked to put saliva on.

The ingenious devices, created by the University of Newcastle in NSW, had been commercialised in the early 2020's by an Australian biotech company and had revolutionised testing for diabetes - allowing patients to stop having to take blood samples to test blood sugars - which could now be reliably tested using saliva and a computer circuit linked to any mobile device like a phone or tablet.

"How are you doing mate?" Damian enquired of his friend.

"Not bad at all" Giacomo replied.

"I'm gradually decreasing my food intake, and the algae seem to be stably producing sugars - turns out the transdermal nutrition scientists were right - we can indeed get simple small molecules like sugars into our bodies this way"

"And how's the temperature?" Damian asked

"That's probably the main worry - I keep spiking, because my sweat glands have basically stopped working. It's a bit like those old movies where they painted people's skin with gold paint, and a couple of people died before they realised they needed to leave a bare patch on the back" Giacomo explained.

"But the ice jackets and keeping the room below 20 degrees is working ok"

"Well we'll have to work out that issue, because there will be people in tropical countries with no access to air conditioning" Damian noted.

"I'm thinking we use some kind of anti-algal treatment for sections of the skin - maybe the back, or chest. Perhaps if we just have the areas of skin usually exposed like arms and legs it will be enough?" Giacomo said.

"Good idea" Damian dictated this into his recorder for further research.

"Ok, if you're feeling up to it, how about we take a turn along the boardwalk" - It would be good to keep getting you outside for a short time each day, beyond just sitting in the sunlight."

"Sure mate, that would be good" Giacomo agreed.

For the next week or so, Damian and Giacomo kept up the routine of a daily trip out along the boardwalk which formed the first part of the walk to Shelley Beach. Whilst the wheelchair couldn't be taken down the steps to the beach, there was about half a kilometre of boardwalk and then flat ground running out by old gun emplacements.

One day, as they sat in a small hanging swamp area, about 300 metres from the start of the walk, Giacomo's monitoring display started beeping, and as Damian watched, several of the measurements spiked and then fell back into the green zone.

Damian coked his head to the side like a dog that has just been whistled by his master.

"Hand on a sec, what just happened there" he said to no-one in particular.

As he finished asking the rhetorical question, the measurements spiked and then went green again. Then in a rhythm of a few seconds, the measurement spiked again and again, each time returning to normal.

Giacomo, who was also watching the display carefully by now, said "it looks like an engine trying to restart - there is a definite pattern to it"

Just then Damian noticed a small detail he had missed. "Hey do that again" he said.

"Do what?" Giacomo said.

"You're brushing your hand over that clump of moss on the branch next to you" Damian said.

"Your vitals are changing each time you do it, there is an interaction between you and the other plants"

"Nonsense" Giacomo said, "that's just a coincidence"

"I'm not so sure, but anyway, we had better be getting back. I'm going to look into it." Damian replied.

"I was re-watching a David Attenborough show the other night. He was measuring sound frequencies that changed when a bee flew near a flower, and I think there is something here we need to find out"

Over the next couple of days, they alternated a stroll along the boardwalk, with Damian pushing Giacomo along with now closed roads up to the lookouts at the top of the quarantine reserve.

Giacomo continued to do well, except for some continuing trouble with temperature control, and that unusual pattern of readings whenever he reached out and touched a bush, or tree branch.

As it turned out, Damian didn't get a chance to investigate those strange patterns. One afternoon, whilst back in his room after a walk, Giacomo's condition took a turn for the worse and he developed a lung infection, which turned into pneumonia.

A day or two later, he went into a coma, and never recovered consciousness.

Giacomo passed away in the middle of September.

A memorial service was held on the base, attended by all base personnel and every scientist.

His body was not laid to rest, due to the unusual circumstances, but Giacomo had already identified in his will that he wanted his body donated to the continuing research project.

Damian and Marietta were as expected heartbroken, but as the project had to continue, they suppressed their grief and continued on with their work - which was reaching a level of desperation now that Giacomo's sacrifice had not led to the happy ending that his life of good humour surely deserved

**Storm Clouds**

**October 2024**

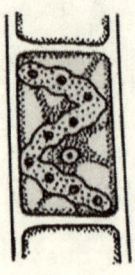

Her hand slowly slipped down the glass of the lab door as she sunk to the ground, only inches from him, but as good as being the other side of the universe for all he could do to reach her.

Her temperature had spiked only minutes before and with the lab going into automatic lock down, Damian had not had time to get to the doors to the lab to help her.

His wife of 25 years was in serious trouble and there wasn't a damn thing he could do to save her.

Noooooooo! He shouted and sank to the floor himself.

His colleagues found him there a few minutes later, when the room alarm triggered a base wide alert.

He was just staring into space, tears rolling down his face.

The base lab doors were eventually opened when a security code was entered, and once the automated bio screening determined there was no threat.

Marietta was unconscious when Damian reached her side.

"Marietta! Marietta!!" he held her arm checking for a pulse, counting in his head and then whispering urgently to his wife as he sat by her side.

As he sat there, the doctors arrived with a gurney and a code blue kit.

"She has a pulse - fast, over 100 beats a minute" Damian said. "We need to get her stabilised" he added.

"Sure, no worries, I'll take it from here, the base physician said"

He took charge of getting Marietta moved onto the gurney and then transferred to a bed in the base hospital. The medical team got to work on stabilising her.

Damian paced up and down outside the hospital ward, nervously looking in to the room as they worked on her.

They did the usual things you'd expect in an intensive care - putting in lines for fluids, connecting her up to the testing machines - heart, lungs etc.

It was different in the fact they also had to monitor what was happening with the photosynthetic organs growing on her skin, and whether she was also rejecting the plant and viral material like had occurred with Damian.

Marietta hadn't had any childhood illnesses like Leukaemia, so her white blood cell system wasn't as sensitive as Giacomo's, but all human bodies were amazing at protecting the body from the threat of organisms - as long as they had antibodies for it. Some cells weren't recognised by the body as a threat - but once a threat was identified, the body was quick to act with the increased production of white blood cells, and other healing activities.

Increased body temperature was just one symptom that would often tell you the body was fighting an infection.

The question was, could Marietta pull through.

She had been left a lot longer than anyone would have liked with no monitoring or support - and Damian wasn't sure. He hoped, but he also had Giacomo's situation as a reminder that this sort of experiment was all kinds of tough for the human body to cope with.

His wife was tough but was she tough enough.

"She's stable" The physician said at last, over an hour later.

"Is she going to be ok?" Damian said nervously.

"I just don't know. We only have the experience with Giacomo to guide us in regards to the algae colony and rejection" The physician answered.

"I wish i had better news but she will be ok for now, and we think will be out of the coma in about 6-8 hours. We'll keep her under until we can be sure she is stably stable if you know what I mean"

"Ok, what should I do then?" Damian was at a loss right now, and everything else had been banished from his mind in the worry about his wife.

"May I suggest if at all possible, you get some sleep for a few hours" The physician answered

"Both Marietta and all of us need you rested and ready to continue the fight for survival" He added.

"Ok Doc" Damian said. I'll try.

"I can prescribe something to help if you want"

"No thanks, I'll take some melatonin, but I don't want any drugs in my system at the moment"

"Ok, I understand"

And with that, he shepherded Damian out of the room, and continued busying himself with his work checking on Marietta's vitals, and hanging new bags of fluids.

Damian reluctantly walked from the room, and headed past the commissary to try and eat some food although he had little appetite.

He managed to eat a little and mixed up a melatonin supplement and then took himself to bed, where he slept fitfully for a few hours at least.

Over the following weeks, Damian was by Marietta's side almost continually.

He had a cot moved into the Intensive Care room.

Marietta was brought out of the coma and eventually she was well enough to move into an isolation unit, and then to return to light duties.

From then on the couple worked on data, and measurements and kept hacking away at the problem.

They had banned anyone other than one physician, a nurse and the couple from coming into the room in case there was any cross infection from the viral transport.

Every day was approached as if it was her last, and this weighed heavily on Damian's mind, but he stayed silent with his thoughts and pushed them back in his mind to focus on the problem.

One morning, Marietta said "I'm not sure I have much time left".

Damian drew in a short breath, it caught in his throat and he tried to speak but couldn't.

Eventually he calmed his thumping heart enough to speak.

"Nonsense, we're going to beat this" he replied.

"We need a plan if we can't" she insisted.

Then something clicked into place for Damian, like a bolt out of the blue.

"Actually, you know what" he said. "I actually think I have one"

With that he called the physician, and instructed him to clear everyone away from the start of the bush walking area they all loved so much.

"What are we doing?" Marietta asked.

"We're going for a walk" he said.

Damian helped Marietta into a wheelchair and took her out to the hanging swamp.

"Something I noticed with Giacomo, but never got a chance to follow up on" Damian finally explained once they were sitting out in the hanging swamp area.

"What do you mean?" Marietta said.

"I noticed a chance in Giacomo's vitals every time he reached out and touched a bush or tree branch" Damian added.

"Can you reach out and touch that plant" he asked.

Marietta did so, stroking the leaves of the native grass next to her and almost immediately they both noticed a change in the pattern of various measurements on her display screen.

"Interesting", Marietta said.

"I actually feel a little calmer at the same time" she added.

"What do you mean?" Damian asked.

"Well, it's hard to tell, but there is a definite feeling of a flow of energy from that plant" she replied.

Over the next hour, they tested this on multiple different plants and the change in patterns continued.

"Well I think that's enough empirical observation for me" Damian concluded after a little while.

"I agree" Marietta said. "There is a connection between the plants and the algae/viral system on my skin"

"Let's get inside and do some more observations, but I know what we need to do now" Damian said.

"We just have to work out some kind of diversion" he added.

"Well there is one diversion that is obvious" she replied.

**Macquarie University Chapel**

**December 2024**

The minister put on his reading glasses and looked over his notes.

The university chapel was filled to overflowing, faculty and students alike ashen faced, many holding Kleenex or wiping aways tears.

Marietta had been a faculty member for over fifteen years, and an alumni of the university for twenty five.

She was the most famous graduate of the Sciences Faculty and had brought attention and funding to the third and youngest of Sydney's well credentialed universities.

But more than that, she was known to all, a mentor to many, and a close friend to dozens of people on the Campus.

"It is a solemn occasion that brings us together to farewell one of our own" - the minister began.

Damian sat in the front row, with a friend from the lab next to him, and both his wife's and his families around him.

He was present in body, but not really in spirit. That had left him when Marietta had left the lab.

He stared at the minister, occasionally turning his attention to the small table in the front of the chapel, carrying his wife's picture.

On the table appropriately were native flowers from the bushland around the University and from the Blue Mountains - gum leaves, sprigs of wattle, a banksia or two.

Her ashes were also there in a box made from Sydney Red Gum - they would be scattered off the pathways of the National Pass, which was also appropriate to Marietta's wishes.

A series of speakers got up and gave readings from both spiritual texts and also quotes from well known naturalists and botanics.

At the end of the service, Damian walked up, took the small box in hand and left the chapel on his own. Everyone who was there witnessed that shell of a man who left, and their hearts went with him.

He stayed for a while at the wake, held in the Macquarie University Cafe, but he was as expected quiet, withdrawn and his mind elsewhere.

After a while, his friend came over and put a hand on his shoulder - "come on mate, let me take you home"

Surprisingly to his mate, Damian actually looked both calm and serene - an unexpected combination that didn't make sense - His friend concluded that maybe he was just now internalising his emotion and putting on a brave face - but there was something there he couldn't quite put his finger on.

But he put that thought aside, and took the long drive back to the Blue Mountains and dropped Damian at Whispering Pines.

And that was the last time anyone saw Damian for four long years.

Revelation

Whispering Pines

Wentworth Falls

March 2027

The door chimed right on 10.00am at Damian Costa's mountain retreat - Whispering Pines. Set at the end of the road leading to Wentworth Falls - outside Sydney's fringe in the Blue Mountains - this beautiful home had lain empty with overgrown gardens for over 40 years until purchased by Damian and Marietta in the early 2020's.

It was now the home of a recluse, with the original intent to escape the glare of the media following Marietta's Nobel prize win - had now become both prison and escape for Damian.

In fact this was the first time another human being had set foot in the house since her death.

Serena Hamilton-Smith was all business as she stepped into the covered entryway and pressed the front door bell. Dressed in a blue suit, stylish briefcase in hand, combination microphone and video camera on a mini tripod in her hand, she heard a click and the door swung inwards and there was a brief bit of static and then…

"Just come through the hallway into the kitchen and then turn right into the living room" she was instructed by the disembodied voice in the speaker next to the door.

As she walked down the long hallway, she noted a old style book library on the left, filled with scientific journals and botany books. A brief glimpse at a glass display case revealed some exquisite botanical drawings which looked to be signed by Joseph Banks. There were also stacked press books of botanical samples, some antique microscopes and collecting equipment - it was like walking into a mini museum.

As an ex forensics and crime reporter, she had trained herself to observe the tiniest details of any environment, and all of these observations were made in the few seconds as she walked down the hall, looking left and right.

Another small anteroom contained a couple of beautiful old wing back reading chairs, and on side tables next to each were these strange reading lights with round globes topping a tripod of animal horns.

On each side table there was a small stack of books, reading glasses and a little glass domed terrarium with a single small succulent plant inside.

Definitely to the home of a scientist and botanist she concluded - it was a combination of history and living artefacts all to do with the plant kingdom, as would be expected from one of the planet's preeminent living botanical and geneticist science families.

Entering the kitchen, she noted a beautiful glass conservatory room leading off to the left which was filled with all manner of Ferns, Bonsai, African violets, and orchids amongst other strange looking plants from some unknown species.

It seemed to run the length of the back of the house and was possibly an old verandah that had been enclosed from the look of the brick arches spaced evenly along the external wall - now filled with big beautiful glass windows.

She then entered the main living room of the house, her jaw dropped - the scenery from the main room was spectacular looking out across the stunning blue mountains wilderness below the Wentworth Falls.

She walked up to the huge windows and stared into the distance - marvelling at the blue coloured haze for which the mountains were named.

"You know the haze is caused by eucalyptus oil in the air"

Serena spun around to see a middle aged man standing behind her.

"Oh my goodness, you startled me, I didn't hear you come in"

"Well that would have been a feat, since I am a computer projection and didn't walk in! he smiled and added "may I offer you some refreshments? Damian is held up on an international call and he asked me to entertain you for a few minutes until he gets here.

"You're AI? she queried?"

"Yes indeed, although my physical appearance was modelled on a long term friend of Damian's father who was the previous owner of this house back in the 1990's"

Oh, he's had the house for a while then?

"Damian spent some time here as a young teenager, and then after he and Marietta got married he bought the house from his Dad's friend"

"The view is amazing - how far is it to the bottom of the valley"

"It's a little over a thousand metres to the bottom and you can walk all the way down via a staircase near the falls at the end of this street"

"It's basically wilderness all the way to Bowral on the Southern Highlands from here - the national park is nearly 3000 square kilometres"

That's a lot of nature, Serena offered by way of a combination of amazement, admiration and just a little shiver up the back of her neck - she wasn't really the outdoors type, so the walk down to the bottom of the Valley would remain something to be imagined as opposed to being done"

Now then, refreshments?

"Yes, just a green tea would be fine if you have it"

Of course, just a moment.

She heard a small motor start up, and within seconds a plunger style tea pot, cups, saucers, teacake on a tray swung through a small door on what looked like the old Sushi train tracks from another room.

Serena gave another start at the sight of the automated delivery, as she had already almost forgotten that the middle aged man standing in front of her was a computer projection. She had half expected to see him walk out into the kitchen and prepare and walk the tea tray back in to the room.

Just as she was reaching for the tea, another start as the AI projection simply started to fade out as the projectors turned off and the residual light gradually diminished.

"Sorry said the AI" as his voice continued - now disembodied again "not used to having visitors - i'll be back in a moment, I just a query I have to handle for Damians call and the bandwidth doesn't allow projection and calculations at the same time."

Serena smiled, remembering a time not too long ago, when the complaint was getting enough bars on the mobile phone to make a call - it seemed data speed would always be a step behind requirements - no matter the level of technology.

And the Blue Mountains was still a long way from the city, and as she had noted the bottom of Falls Road was a fair way below the mountain highway level of the township.

So despite 9G mobile technology and high speed optical fibre cable, there was still a limit to both processing and transmission speeds.

Serena sat down at a small breakfast table by the window and contemplated the questions she had for Damian, although she had gone over them many times, she somehow felt uneasy about the upcoming interview.

Not surprising given the dramatic events of the last few years, and the fact no one had heard or seen Damian in public for over 3 years - not since the death of his wife in 2024.

Why did she do what she did? What did you feel and think when the CSIRO then the UN and Nobel Prize committee stripped her of the accolades and prizes? Given your combined work saved hundreds of millions, do you think it was fair? What have you been doing the last few years?

The questions tumbled over in her mind as she sipped her tea, and stared without seeing the beauty of the Eucalypt bushland just metres from where she sat.

A muted cackling noise like an engine starting snapped her out of her reverie and she realised a paid of kookaburras were sitting on the branch of a gum tree warming up to their full battle cry - so loved by Australians, and lauded in poetry and stories - the laughing kookaburra sounded more like a chainsaw to Serena.

The two birds held their beaks pointing up and facing opposite directions they continued to cackle away, until they sounded like they were giving up on the effort and it dwindled away to silence again.

Silence was certainly a constant up in the mountains - it must be difficult to sleep up here at night she thought...

...just then the AI appeared again a couple of metres away and commented - we'll they've done their job and established their territory again. He added - it might be called a laugh, but it's like the growl of a tiger or the roar of a lion - it's their way of saying, this is our space keep away"

Then, without a moment's hesitation or waiting for Serena to reply, he moved off the topic of Kookaburras and said

"Damian is ready for the interview now, if you follow me I'll take you to his private study downstairs"

I forgot to ask your name, if you have one? - Serena again feeling like she was talking to a living, breathing person the effect was so real felt she had to make more of a connection.

"It's Alfred, he said offering a small chuckle - Damian was a bit of a fan of Batman as a child, and i was actually given my name by Damian and Marietta's long time university friend and lab colleague - Giacomo - he was the joker in the group"

Serena chuckled and then caught herself thinking she sounded just a little like the kookaburras outside.

"Ok, lead on Alfred, she said"

Alfred moved silently like he was floating on air although his image gave the impression of walking away from her back up the corridor to a door she had somehow missed on the way in - although not surprising since it had the same wood panelling of the rest of the hall, and a very small doorknob that was set into one of the squares.

The door cracked open and Alfred stood there and motioned her in the direction of the stairs - which also had the dark wood panelling all the way down.

An old red runner carpet was pegged into the stairs by brass holders on each vertical face of the step.

It felt like walking into one of those old jazz basements in the city, or perhaps a supper club or speakeasy, she thought as she descended.

She stopped on the fourth or fifth step and looked back to Alfred and said - are you coming?

Alfred shook his head and said — no hologram transmitters on the lower floor - so I'm afraid I won't be accompanying you, but the study is the only room at the bottom, so you can't get lost.

Ok, she said, see you in a while and she turned and continuing moving down the steps to the lower floor.

As she got to the bottom of the stairs, she was presented with another hallway, carrying beautiful old engraving images of trees, and plants and flowers.

Other than the pictures, which has beautiful small brass lights bent over the top to feature each print, there was not a stick of furniture or ornamentation in the hall.

Just the same ornately decorated red hall runner leading up to a completely unexpected metallic door.

Serena reached out and knocked on the door, which was cold to the touch, and it slid silently back into a hidden wall cavity, revealing an equally unexpected steel and glass modern office that wouldn't have been out of place in a co-working space in the city.

At the far end of the room, which was very dim, she spotted a desk and a figure sitting behind it in the dark. She shivered involuntarily, for no good reason.

Come in, she heard Damian say. Excuse the low light, but I have an eye condition and I'm afraid it would almost blind me to lift the light levels in here. I also have a bit of a virus so I don't want you to catch it. My voice is a little croaky so apologies in advance.

If it's ok I'd prefer to sit here in the dark, and you can sit at that chair just there with the spotlight to see your notes and questions.

She felt a little apprehensive and weird, and there was a smell in the room that was a little musty or mouldy - she couldn't quite pick it - it wasn't unpleasant, just a little dank.

"Ok, mmm can I place my recorder on your desk to capture the interview?"

"No need, stay over there, and I'll have Alfred record it on the inbuilt microphones in the room, I use them to record my observations when I'm working here"

"We'll send it to your phone immediately on completion of the interview with a transcription if you like"

"Well that will save me, so thank you that's fine"

"I was hoping to record the interview on video too, she added"

"I'm sorry, but with the eye condition, I'd prefer not if that's ok, but we'll send you some file video and a headshot if you like" he added helpfully.

"ok, I suppose that will have to do"

"We'll see how the interview goes, but if I'm feeling up to it, perhaps we can do a short final video of a minute or two at the end"

"Let's begin shall we" he said by way of moving things along.

"Ok, good" she replied.

"Can we start at the beginning of this particular project - of human bioforming - and tell me where the idea originally came from"

She heard him take a sharp inward breath, and knew it was all still raw for him, and yet he cleared his throat and began filling her in on the history.

The interview continued for another 45 minutes or so, until finally it was complete. Both parties seemed happy about that.

"Well that's it - I asked all my questions, thank you so much for your time" Serena said finally.

"You're most welcome - are you sure there is nothing else you want to know" Damian said, making it clear he had more to offer

"I think I'm done, and I'd have to say I think this profile will encourage people to look a little more warmly on the sacrifices that Marisa and of course Giacomo made." she offered as a summary and conclusion to her thoughts.

"I can send you a draft of the piece if you'd like?" she added.

"No need, I'm happy for you to write it as you see it, and judge us as we deserve, but there is one question you haven't asked" Damian pressed and it was obvious he wanted to add something.

"What would that be?" she said.

"Why did I lock myself away in this home for the past three years?" He offered.

"Well I assumed of course that you lost your wife and that was the reason"

"Well yes of course, but there was also the fact that I wanted to continue our research, you see I was convinced there was an answer and I couldn't stand by and just watch the global population just disintegrate without trying"

"You, you continued the research? She stammered, suddenly feeling ice run through her veins"

"What do you mean, the UN banned the research after the deaths"

"Well yes, but I didn't continue that study, and no further patients were injected with the virus/algal solution after the ban"

"Well what did you continue then, if not that experiment"

"Well this was more of an experiment about how to have a patient survive the first 48 hours - which was the critical time for the body to adjust to the new heat stasis - after which we had hypothesised that a steady state would be achieved and if the core temperature was kept down, perhaps someone could survive"

"But you said no other patients were injected, how could you study this?

She asked tentatively but a horrible thought had already started brewing in her journalistic mind.

"Well, we did have one other test subject"

"Who?" she asked, her fear building

"Perhaps it's time to answer the first question, as to why I became a recluse."

I needed somewhere cool and quiet for the patient, and this house seemed the perfect place.

We had already built the below ground lab under the old house by excavating the original basement and making it substantially larger.

It is also temperature controlled, and has grade 7 biohazard containment and destruction facilities should those be required.

But that is now unlikely, as the patient has been proven to be non-contagious - at least except for this damn cold virus.

"You, you are the patient?" Serena half stammered.

"Why naturally, I wasn't about to let Giacomo and Marisa's sacrifice be in vain and I'm certainly not going to keep someone prisoner here for three years - he laughed croakily and then coughed"

"Well its now time to reveal the results of the work"

"It's been a success, I don't require any nutrition via normal human means, and the air in this part of the world is actually quite invigorating for plants too"

"I'm not sure what you mean"

"In good time"

"I require only water and carbon dioxide, and the green chlorophyll in my skin works nicely to convert that into sugars and amino acids enough for all my needs"

"Of course it's become a bit difficult to move around, and I struggle sometimes with bending over"

"As it turns out, whilst the experiment worked, it isn't really the answer we've been looking for, as we forgot about one little factor.

"And what was that, Serena was now very anxious and actually felt like dropping everything and running out, but she stayed if only to satisfy the journalist in her - because the human was scared shitless"

"Well you see, the viral transport we used worked perfectly, and it helped get the algae and it's chlorophyll right where we wanted it - under the skin"

"Sugar production started within a day or so once I'd passed the steady state on temperature"

"But then it went a bit pear shaped so to speak"

"Ohh?" it was the single gasped word she could get out of her now dry mouth. Serena could literally hear her heart beat pounding in her ears now - so loud it was difficult to hear anything else.

Just then Professor Costa - one half of the most highly decorated botanic and genetics team the world had seen since Charles Darwin pressed a button on his desk with a rather loud click and the illumination in the room gradually started increasing.

She heard him move in his chair and stand up, and then a rustle as he moved around the desk to the side nearest the window.

She let out an involuntary gasp.

"It's quite ok"

"You see I was that final patient, I injected myself in the same way that Giacomo and Marisa did, but for some reason I survived"

"But when the algae started to evolve, triggered by something in my own genetic makeup, it rapidly moved through the whole evolutionary tree of the plant kingdom, stopping at the pinnacle of evolution - the flowering trees"

Her heart beating, but now strangely unafraid as he had revealed himself.

His skin was like a mat of leaves, glowing green in the afternoon sun from the window. On his body, a gnarled yet smooth bark seemed to have formed on his chest, shoulders.

He was wearing dark trousers, but no shirt.

His feet poked out of the bottom of the trousers, and it looked for all the world like his feet had begun turning into roots - with longish tendrils coming from each of the five points where his toes may have once been.

"Soon the transformation will continue beyond the point where I can easily move about - he said"

Then it will be time to go.

"But where will you go, Serena asked, now calm, yet concerned for him"

"I'll sort something out" Damian said in a tone that communicated he wouldn't go into it further.

"But I allowed your interview because I do have a message I'd like to share, and now if you would do me a favour and set up the video? he asked"

"Of course, she said"

**Television Studios - Channel 9**

**Sydney, Australia**

**Sunday Night, March 14th 2029**

Serena took a look over her notes as the makeup team fussed over last minute touch ups to her face.

The lights felt hotter than usual, but perhaps that was just her apprehension at delivering this particular story.

Her co-host looked over and smiled, saying nothing but obviously noticing her distress.

She half smiled back, but her face felt tight, and itchy from the makeup - and she waved the team away.

"That will have to do, you're making me nervous" She added "I'm sorry, it's not you, I'm just tense.

She heard the news director in her ear - "live in 10, 9, 8, 7..."

Serena took one last huge breath, hoping to calm her nerves, but it didn't really work - her heart was still about to burst through her chest.

"Focus on the first sentence, you'll be right from there" she said quietly to herself.

She looked up and found camera 1, as the voice in her ear counted down '4,3,2...'

Hello, my name is Serena Hamilton-Smith and tonight I want to share the story of Professors Marisa and Damian Costa. Two people who dedicated their lives to solving the problem of world food shortages - only to be vilified for moving too fast with their experiments to bioform the human race.

On one hand, Nobel Prize winners for saving hundreds of millions of lives. On the other, sacrificing their lives to save billions more, but being excommunicated from both scientific and global circles when people said they went too far.

Perhaps it's true, but there's a side of the story you don't know.

How Damian didn't give up and become a recluse after his wife's death.

He continued to try to find a solution and in the end sacrificed his own life, just as she had done.

In the search for an answer in human bioforming.

In the end, the results of that research and his viewpoint on it, can only really come from the man himself, not from observers who didn't put it all on the line.

Professor Costa now believes we should NOT try to Bioform ourselves - he thinks we should explore other avenues.

Why?

Well I think i'd better just let you hear that from Damian himself in his last interview before his death this last week.

She and Damian had agreed to keep his retirement a secret and to 'close the book' so to speak with this last interview.

And so at 6.55pm on that night, the world saw what the man had become.

Half man, half plant - the next step in our evolution or a divergence that could or should not be permitted!

In the end, whilst he was transformed, Serena still felt that the human side remained - his love of exploration, of science and his love of humanity - a deep seated philanthropy giving beyond what anyone had given before.

**Epilogue**
**Somewhere in the Blue Mountains**
**Sydney, Australia**
**March 25th 2029**

Damian stepped carefully off the rocks at the bottom of the mountain pass.

He walked slowly and carefully, like an old man with limited flexibility in his limbs left.

In Damian's case, this was far more than arthritis or muscle aches - his skin now literally transformed into a mix of bark and leaf like textures - the photosynthesis now provided the bulk of his nutrient intake - the rest came from a special protein supplement that he and Marietta had developed.

He walked for some time, and eventually turned off the main tracks and headed deep into the subtropical rainforest - a remnant of a million years old forest that previously had covered the entire region.

He came to a small clearing after some time - no evidence of his passing from the track into the forest remained.

He knew this clearing well - with its little clear brook and running water coming over the large worn sandstone boulders. He could even now see a couple of large freshwater yabbies in the middle of the pond - their shells a mix of green and blue.

He felt some added empathy for them now, and whilst they would be able to discard their hardened shell every so often as they grew - this was a luxury he did not have.

He was now stuck in his weird half plant skin for the remainder of his life.

A life that would be a lot longer than perhaps he had inferred to the journalist during the interview.

Now his condition has stabilised and the anti-rejection medicine was no longer needed - there was no reason why he wouldn't live out the full life expectancy of any man his age - perhaps even longer - depending on how the slowed respiration, heart beat and the nutrient coming from the photosynthesis impacted his longer term health and physical condition.

As he stood by the brook, looking into the water, there was movement on the other edge of the clearing.

Shadows breaking away from shadows and incredibly well camouflaged Damian thought to himself - something that would come in handy.

The smaller shadows now formed into recognisable human shapes as they separated from the main shadows of the trees.

A dozen or more came towards him, and now they were closer he could recognise each individual - members of his original research team from the North Head Quarantine station - all transformed like himself.

And all surviving well in this pre-arranged meeting place.

And now one of the group came closer, and he smiled.

His wife Marietta, back by his side.

"Hi Darling, i'm glad you made it safely" she said, hooking an arm in his.

"Yep, all good, interview done, house secured and no trace left" He confirmed to her, and also loud enough for his colleagues to hear as well.

"Good, then it's time to discuss what's next" Marietta said as the others gathered around them.

Marietta had not perished as the rest of the world thought - she had got through a short period of danger in a semi-comatose state, and when Damian had taken charge of her body at the lab, he had not in fact handed her over to the morgue.

Once they had worked out that the best treatment for the patient was being in a complete outdoor ecosystem, rather than an isolation lab.

Damian and Marietta had faked her death, and he had taken her and cared for her and the others from the mountains lab - and they had lived in the location together for 3 years.

After the lab and project had been closed down, Damian had one by one spoken to the individual scientists and they had all eagerly signed up for the new experiment.

They had been keeping tabs on the entire group and ensuring everyone's continuing health right up until a week before the interview.

They had spent a lot of time as a group, and searched out this location and agreed it would be a good spot for their staged disappearance.

There was water, a mild climate, a large undiscovered cave system nearby on the escarpment. It was there they had provisioned a campsite, a field lab, and everything else they would need for at least five years in the wilderness - maybe more.

Without the need for food supplies, it was surprising how small the cache needed to be.

Even now, as the group moved back to their daily activities, Damian and Marietta could see that the group was guaranteed a long and prosperous future.

They worked so well together, almost without the need for verbal communication.

The wave forms and patterns seen on the medical displays when Giacomo and Marietta touched the plants back in the quarantine area had turned out to be exactly what Damian and Marietta thought they were - communication.

Almost below detection, and certainly beyond the limits of normal human experience, there was indeed a flow of information between plants in this ecosystem.

And now the team had tapped into those flows, they were operating as a true group - individuality was there, but subsumed to the overall needs of the group.

Survival was assured because all their goals were aligned. And it went broader than the group of course. They also understood the roles of each plant and indeed animals in this ecosystem.

They could see the patterns, they could see the roles, they could see the solutions.

Damian smiled as he saw his fellow scientists get back into the activities in which they had been engaged when he arrived.

Some preparing shelters, some conducting measurements and experiments. Others soaking in the late afternoon sunlight, whilst they lounged by the small mountain stream that ran through the glade.

Everyone else in the group had left the mountain home and come here, awaiting his arrival.

He has followed after he tidied up the loose ends that would free them from any attention from the world's media, the UN and anyone else.

In any event, it was appropriate, since all those organisations and people were human organisations, and this group was now a group of outsiders, no longer full members of the genus homo sapiens.

So they would continue their existence here, in the middle of one of the worlds largest national parks, in an area rarely visited by walkers or campers.

And they would learn all about their new condition and what living meant to them now - together a group who tried to save humanity and instead created a new species.

And once they understood that, they would then be able to re-introduce themselves to the rest of the world, and perhaps finally solve the main problem they had tackled.

And end to world hunger. An end to starvation. But that would have to wait until another day. Let the search begin.

The End.

Bonus Short Story

# Diaspora

HUNTER LEONARD

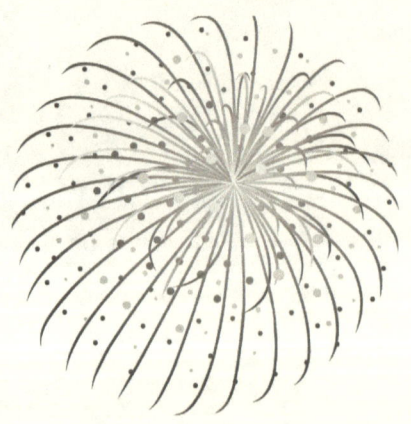

# Prologue

The small winged craft descended through the atmosphere of the large rocky planet - codename Gliese 832 C - popularly called Hermes - it was named after the Greek god  Hermes. Hermes - the god, not the planet - was also god of boundaries or transgression of boundaries - and this was apt given the huge boundary that humankind was about to cross.

The craft was named Diaspora 1 and had been launched from an orbiting platform about 200 miles above Earth almost exactly 100 years prior in 2070. Diaspora 1 had been accelerated to approximately 20% of the speed of light using a photonic propulsion system originally designed by NASA Scientist Phillip Lubin in the early 21st Century.

By the time 2070 came around, small unmanned craft with artificial intelligence on board had been flitting around the Solar System and to nearby Alpha Centauri and Proxima Centauri - a mere several light years from earth.

Much had been learned about Earth's neighbouring stars and planets, but eventually, despite the promise of hundreds of thousands of habitable planets, fewer had been found than expected.

And some, like Gliese 832 C, which had not been a high value 'terrestrial target' had not only been found to be habitable, but actually contained a thriving and abundant ecosystem of plants and animals when the initial fast push craft had done a fly by in 2060.


Diaspora 1 contained the consciousness of one Professor Judith McEwan, originally from Inverness Scotland, latterly of the planet

Earth, and now one of the first humans to reach a planet beyond the home solar system.

If human was a word that could still be applied in this case…

**Launch Day**

The Michelle Obama Transit Station - in geosynchronous orbit above the Eastern United States - June 16th, 2070

The door opened and a mature woman walked slowly into the room. She calmly met the eyes of the scientist already seated at a small conference table.

Before the door slid shut with a light hiss behind her, a rotating walkway could be seen, with a view screen looking down on the North American continent. The planet was moving slowly in one direction, opposite to that of the spinning walkway.

Once the door closed however, the room felt and looked like any medical lab on solid Earth.

The woman moved over to a desk, at which was seated a middle aged man in a body tight white uniform. He had a friendly expression on his face, with piercing blue eyes, and whilst his hair was going slightly grey on the sides, he still looked youthful and fit.

"Good morning Doctor" she said.

"Good morning Professor" he replied with obvious warmth and respect.

The Professor, and her colleague began to chat about the incredible procedure she was about to undergo.

Professor Judith McEwan had worked her entire career at Edinburgh University where she followed triple paths of research in spirituality and neurology and exoplanetology. Judy, as she preferred her colleagues to call her, had been the first to propose what was considered a fantastical notion to many, not only her colleagues in the medical profession, but in any field even slightly interested in philosophy, spirituality, space and life itself.

Judy was considered brilliant, but her reputation was the only thing that had prevented more people labelling her a quack.

For one thing, she had pioneered revolutionary treatment that solved degenerative memory diseases like Dementia by finding that people with these diseases had not lost their minds or memories at all. She identified that the connection between the human soul or spirit had been blocked by a simple coding error in an amino acid in the brain as they aged.

It had also turned out that memories were not actually stored in the physical brain but in some dimensional lattice outside of normal physical space and time. A sort of "mind " subspace for those who were fans of the 20th Century shows like Star Trek.

The leap from finding where the 'mind' or consciousness was, and the ability to dream of a way to move it from one body to another had been a miracle of ingenuity.

"We can bottle the human consciousness and send it to explore other planets." she had said, back in 2048. A quote that was now as famous(or infamous depending on your point of view) as any from Einstein, Watson & Crick or Archimedes.

Professor McEwan had then set about dedicating her life to finding a practical means of doing just that - completely turning the idea of space exploration on its head in the middle of the 21st Century.

No more worrying about stasis pods, or life support. No more worrying about how to cross the enormous distances of space to explore exoplanets.

No more worrying about achieving light speed in space craft - although this final puzzle had been solved anyway and ended up being the simplest thing to solve.

It was only fitting then that Professor McEwan would be amongst the first 1000 people to have their consciousness downloaded and sequestered on micro spacecraft propelled by lasers to the nearest rocky exoplanet in search of new places for the human race to settle.

Their journey would take over 100 years for the spacecraft, equating to a little more than that for those back on earth. Time dilation wasn't a major factor at 20% the speed of light.

It was truly a remarkable moment in the history of humanity, and a redefinition of what it meant to be human.

"Do you have anything you wanted to cover with me, before we start the procedure?" said the doctor.

"Well not really, I'm sure I've trained you well enough by now" she said smiling.

The two of them had been working together for some months now on refining the procedure to literally download or more correctly connect the consciousness into a crystalline matrix - a data cube that could survive virtually anything space could throw at it, short of flying directly into a star of course.

What should have been a sad moment - Professor McEwan had been diagnosed with a rare bone disease recently - was actually one of joy. The essence of who she was - would survive - in the form of what had been variously called the soul, the life force or the spirit by philosophers and religions for many thousands of years.

The small crystal cube would then be loaded into a micro spacecraft that would be propelled up to a speed just short of the speed of light for its journey to the exoplanet.

The small craft would be powered not by engines requiring fuel, but by a combination of a laser beam and a novel gravomag drive - the laser beam providing the impetus or force to move the craft and the gravomag drive performing the role of both navigation and also help with slingshotting the space craft past planets and stars which it would encounter on its journey.

"I guess I have just one last question about the process at the other end when we arrive" she said.

"Well that question is probably fully answered by the engineers" he said "but i can give you an overview" he added

"That would be good" she replied.

"The space craft will also be carrying programmed microbots" he commenced his explanation.

"These will be released on arrival and which will extract the necessary elements from the local rock to replicate themselves and build a 3-D printing machine."

"It is somewhat surprising how simple the atomic makeup of a human body is in terms of chemicals, and because we're not recreating an actual living organism, but a humanoid body so to speak, we can mimic all of the functions need for vision, locomotion and so forth with even the most basic mix of carbon, silicon, calcium and a few other metals and minerals. The 3-D printer is produced first, and then we mine for the ingredients and print you a new body."

"Well seems simple enough, I hope I remember your response in a hundred years" she smiled and also laughed lightly.

"It would have seem inconceivable to talk about life in terms of hundreds of years just a few decades ago" she added with that light Scottish lilt in her voice that everyone who listened to her found both charming and engaging at the same time.

"I agree, and it is quite amazing what the AI programs have been able to come up with in terms of solutions based on your original concepts" he acknowledged

"Ok, well let's get on with it" she said and stood up from the table, eager to be on her way.

"Ok, let's do that" he said.

And with that they moved from the clinic into the next room.

Here was a seat with blue gel pads on the base and back of the seat. Behind the seat was a headset like device hanging from a thin frame.

Wires ran down the frame and snaked across the floor and then up onto the table.

A low table next to the seat contained a series of machines including what looked like, and was in fact an old time oscilloscope plus a data storage unit. In the data storage unit was a small glowing crystal in the shape of a capsule. It was lit from below and gave off a beautiful blue colour. There were no facets on the crystal - it was see through and seemed to be absolutely perfect inside with no inclusions or fractures.

The crystal to be used as a storage vessel for Professor McEwan's consciousness was in fact a manufactured Sapphire - her favourite gem stone.

Professor McEwan sat down on the seat and pushed herself back from the edge into a comfortable position with her head resting lightly on the gel pads.

"Ok, are you ready" said Doctor Patterson.

"I am ready Jamie, and thank you" Judy replied, squeezing his hand in a final touch of affection for a man who had at first been her junior registrar; then professional colleague and after many years, a dear friend.

It was also to be her last moment of human touch, and at that thought, she had a momentary bittersweet feeling of loss. And yet at the same time a growing sense of excitement for the journey ahead.

"Ok, I'm going to place the transfer helmet on your head, and then once the crystal is activated, you can begin." Jamie said.

This was a procedure completed in a fully conscious state. There were no drugs, no anaesthesia.

It had been found in their research, that a suitably trained individual could simply decide for their consciousness to be in a different location and it would instantaneously occur.

In some older cultures, like the Australian Aboriginals, a person was known to be able to will themselves to death.

What hadn't been known was that these cultures had always believed the soul was simply moving on to the next stage in their existence.

And so the Professor has learnt to put her consciousness into the crystal, and had done so many times in preparation for this final and permanent transfer.

She closed her eyes for the last time, and concentrated on the image of the blue sapphire, and in an instant she was there.

Her body would continue to operate as if it was on a life support machine for a few minutes. Enough time for the clinicians to place the now empty shell on a life support machine in case of any misadventure with the launch of the micro ship.

After the crystal transfer, Jamie took it into the neighbouring launch bay. He placed the crystal into one of a thousand small ships which were waiting on small silver rails all lined up and pointing to a large portal.

As Professor McEwan was the last to be transferred, all was now ready for the launch.

Jamie keyed his communicator and confirmed the transfer with the Mission Commander who immediately swung her team into action.

Ok, everyone, let's do this.

"Recorders on"

"Align Helium-Neon laser generators"

"And open the portal please"

The rectangular portal slid open revealing a dark patch of sky peppered with small points of light. As they were in outer space, there was no atmosphere to make the stars 'twinkle'.

One of these small points of light was their destination - the star around which Hermes orbited.

Once the portal was fully open and secure it would stay that way for over one hundred years, a force field protecting the laser machines which would push the machines to their destination.

Inside the launch communications room, several technicians peered carefully at large holographic screens.

"Confirmation of status green please."

All the technicians responded and pressed their status buttons to light up the master holographic display in front of the Commander.

"Ok turn on the lasers to 1% power"

A large dial appeared in front of her on the screen.

"Now set automated power up, and release the holding clamps on the micro ships"

A blur of movement. A dial gradually building with a central number increasing up to 100%.

It was a thing of beauty.

Like a thousand butterflies simultaneously dropping from a tree into glorious flight.

The micro ships were each pushed along the silver rails and out into space, with a thin red beam directed at them. As they left the hatch, small and beautiful umbrella like wings opened up to increase the capture surface for the laser beam.

They also rotated like a bullet leaving a gun barrel, in order to maximise stability on the first few kilometres of their journey.

The room erupted in cheers, echoed by billions all over the world, who were glued to screens small and large to watch this incredible moment in human history.

It would be their grandchildren who would celebrate the completion of the journey a century later, but all who witnessed it were uplifted and the earth experienced a long period of peace and tranquility because of it.

# The Journey

Without a body to worry about, it had been found the human consciousness or spirit could quite easily survive years without real need of external stimulus or entertainment. It would be like a long dream, yet with a constant awareness of 'self'.

Despite there being no need in terms of survival or health of the individual, it was possible for the occupant to communicate with the ship to check progress, or to receive data on interesting sites during the journey such as comets, or star nurseries or any number of astronomical phenomena.

It was also possible for the 'person' to tackle projects of interest, explore subjects of study; and to consider philosophies such as questions on the nature of life and existence.

And of course, they could study data and information about the planet that they were hurtling towards at close to 20% of the speed of light or in layman's terms, more than 215 million kilometres per hour.

# The Arrival

Due to the small size of the craft, no parachutes or rockets were required to land the craft. Also, because the payload was near indestructible, there was little to worry about in terms of the landing.

Nevertheless a small pump inflated a ball like structure around the craft to provide a buffer just in case. The pump operated by pulling in air during the descent and automatically compressing it ready to inflate the ball just before landing.

The craft had been slowing down for nearly a month prior to orbital insertion. Slowing down the craft required a combination of dialling back the power of the laser and also reversing the gravomag drive to utilise local gravity and magnetic waves to wash off speed - much like airbrakes might be used on a ground vehicle.

The tiny craft finally hit on the surface of the planet and bounced a couple of times before coming to rest in a small depression on a sandy strip of land near a lake, filled with a cloudy, sky blue liquid.

The ball around the craft deflated and drew back into its compartment.

Six small strut like legs folded out from the craft, and swivelled to point down at the ground. They pushed down into the ground, and once a firm footing was confirmed sections of the legs telescoped out to lift the craft about 3 inches off the surface.

At this point a small door opened and a small sprinkle of a metallic dust-like substance drifted down the three inches between the belly of the craft and the sandy ground.

These were actually the microscopic robots which would now begin the task of recovering silicon and other minerals from the sand to prepare the 3D print.

Each microbot had its own role in the sequence with dozens of them carrying redundant backups of each instruction in case of any damage or loss to a single bot.

Over the next few hours, they replicated themselves as well as began the process of creating the printer. And a long silver framework began to form on the ground right next to the craft.

It took a total of 24 hours for the microbots to harvest the necessary ingredients and to finalise the printer. The pace got faster and faster as they replicated more and more bots, and more and more materials.

The genius of the program came to its fore when the bots had virtually completed the framework, and then they joined together to form the operating system of the printer, completing a wireless link to the ship and transporting the crystal cube into position prior to the android body printing process.

Whilst the printer was being finalised, a second group of bots was conducting initial surveys of the ground and atmospheric makeup of the landing site.

This data was being fed into the ships computer and translated into Judy's consciousness so she was also aware of the situation she would find herself in once the body was completed.

Not that there was any survival issues, since the humanoid body was a transport device not a life raft so to speak.

However, an understanding of the conditions and terrain were important for the final specifications of the body to ensure Judy could move around easily. Other elements that were important included the light spectrum for image capture, sound levels for audio and various other environmental analytics.

**A new beginning.**

Judy opened her eyes and saw only an indigo coloured sky, with narrow streaks of jet black clouds running vertically across it.

The resolution of the twin image capture devices was rather remarkable she thought immediately. It was however somewhat disorientating, because despite the high technology, they weren't human eyes.

Judy put her attention onto the rest of her body, feeling servos begin to spin at key joints as she focused in on fingers and toes, and then arms and legs.

She also felt the warmth of the various fluids cycling around her body through small artery like tubes. These fluids would keep servos lubricated, and would also wash any micro particles of dust or dirt which made its way into the body.

Judy checked out the operating systems via the on board computer which functioned like an automatic subservient mind under her conscious control. Satisfied all was in order, she lifted one arm and swung the printer boom up and away from the body.

She then sat up, and then rolled over and pushed herself to a standing position for the first time in her new body.

Standing erect, she perceived the gravity below her feet and the weight of the body being pulled down towards the centre of the planet.

She also felt the fairly strong wind against sensors in the outer surface of the body, which was covered in a lattice like exoskeleton to protect the inner workings of the mechanism.

Perceptions meant survival in a flesh and blood body. Yet they were still important here in order for full analysis of the surrounding environment, and for keeping her body further protected and oriented during the survey mission.

They were also a comfort to Judy, and she was glad the body specifications had been included to ensure there was no disconnection from the physical environment of the planet, which would have made the survey task less real to her.

She looked around and could immediately see other ships and printers in various stages of completion in the hundred yards or so around her.

She was indeed standing on the sandy shore of a lake, as the computer had indicated upon landing.

As the first ship to land - an honour bestowed upon her for this mission - her body had been completed around 8 hours prior to the other colonists.

This meant she had some time to walk around the area and soak in the fact that she had finally arrived and become the first human to set foot on a planet outside the home solar system.

Professor Judith McEwan then took a moment before completing a rather simple, yet time honoured tradition that humankind had adopted for its missions off planet.

A tradition that began with those famous words uttered by Neil Armstrong, via a static filled radio signal when he became the first man to set foot on the moon.

Her humanoid body had a programmed voice, but the voice they heard back on Earth would be a recording of her own physical, flesh and blood vocal chords uttering those same words over one hundred years prior and saved for this very moment.

She instructed the computer to begin playing the recording for her mind only - to be repeated once all the colonist explorers were ambulant in a few hours. This, in harmony with the same recording being played across the entire Earth, and all other home solar system colonies.

"I, Professor Judith McEwan, the first female consciousness of human kind to land on a planet outside our solar system, hereby declare our colony's safe arrival on the planet Hermes. Like the Greek God for which this planet is named, I send a message of hope for humanity. May this first small step for women, a giant leap for humankind, spark a new diaspora for all that is good in our species - intelligence, curiosity, tolerance, love and most of all, creativity. May whatever deity you worship, whatever inspiration you draw on, whatever goal you desire - be firmer and more real in your mind today"

And with that, Judy turned and started the short walk along the cloudy blue stream over grey sandy soil towards the ships of the other colonists.

It was time to begin. The End.

Second Bonus

# UFB

by

Hunter Leonard

# UFB

The blacked out windows of the train carriage gave it a menacing look at the station. Significantly enhanced by the squad of soldiers standing all around it, holding futuristic looking automatic weapons. Each soldier was a carbon copy of the other - muscled, short buzz cut hair and green berets marking them as special forces.

While they waited, ramrod straight and staring blankly from their posts, a small group of bespectacled science types stood around a long metal container - sprayed a dull white colour.

From the box came a low humming courtesy of the refrigeration unit attached to the box, keeping the contents frozen.

A chill wind blew through the station situated just outside the secret installation south of Fairbanks, Alaska. The science types wrapped their arms around their chests, trying to keep some warmth in their hands. The special forces squad to a man did not move a muscle.

A door in the carriage slid open with a mechanical hiss and as it completed its slide back inside the skin of the special train carriage, a second glass door was revealed. Behind this another science type individual stood calmly. She was tall, probably mid to late forties, and wearing a lab coat with goggles pulled down around her neck.

She reached out and touched the wall next to her, and the glass door also slid back into the interior of the train carriage.

Without the reflecting glass, an observer could now see inside to a fully equipped lab.

Without saying a word, she nodded at the closet soldier who barked an order and 4 of his men responded, slipping guns over shoulders and then lifting the white container up and into the carriage.

They then vaulted into the space, and completed lifting the container up onto a carrying stand in the middle of the lab.

They immediately turned, jumped down to the ground and resumed their positions around the train.

The door closed on the freezer unit, the lab, and the scientist.

The other group of scientist turned around and moved away whilst the soldiers stood their posts.

Inside, the female scientist moved over to the container.

She pressed on a small button on the top.

A small hiss.

A child's face.

Serene and beautiful.

Discovered in the permafrost of an Alaskan wilderness, the female child was thought to be approximately 8 or 9 years old when she died. Almost ten thousand years before.

She had not died of natural causes, being murdered by her tribe because she was different

She of the blonde hair, piercing blue eyes, and remarkable genetics had shown she was immune to the anthrax like virus which had struck down 58% of the world's population since it was released from melting permafrost and carried on winds around the globe.

This beautiful child had lived during the same time period as that virus, and she carried antibodies for it.

Hence the security.

And the care.

For this child of the past, was now the future.

Third Bonus

# Hex 31b

by

Hunter Leonard

# Hex 31 - B

The year: 2231

The location: Milky Way Galaxy, Orion Spur, approximately two hundred light years from Earth.

"I'm sorry Captain, but your request to dock at our planetary receiving centre has been denied" intoned the deep voice emanating from the Orions bridge speakers.

"May I ask why?" questioned Captain Lou Delamonte.

"We're not accepting Humans at this time" replied the voice, which belonged to the senior Aide to the Ambassador of Hex-31b (the human designation for this planet)

"What do you mean at this time?" the Captain persisted.

"For the foreseeable future" the Aide added.

"You see Captain, your species is really, altogether too much trouble, what I mean to say is well, er, you just don't see to want to fit in" said the Aide, obviously uncomfortable at being challenged beyond his first response.

"Oh I see, too much trouble eh" commented the Captain tersely.

"Well thanks for nothing"

The Captain turned to the navigator.

"Helm, turn us around, and lay in a course for the next star system please"

Having a reputation for trouble was now becoming troubling for Captain Delamonte. His mission, as defined by the governing Humanity Council was to find suitable places for the remaining human population.

Earth was long gone, destroyed when the ozone layer finally collapsed some third years previously. The remaining extant human population was on board a fleet of light ships now spreading out from the parched husk - all that was left of humanity's first home.

The entire population of humans was less than ten thousand - all younger than 40 - all selected in a ballot for a place on the light ships.

Once the domain of science fiction writers, the human exodus had become all too real in the latter part of the 23rd Century. Knowing the end was near humanity had lifted as one to research and develop ships that could carry them across the galaxy.

Human's had lifted to solve the technology problems, but their social problems had followed them halfway across Orion's Spur.

The early colonising ships had found intelligent life on other planets, made contact, and proceeded to try and assert control over those that had initially welcomed them with open arms.

Much of this part of the galaxy was populated with advanced civilisations who had long since found peace and harmony within their populations and with their natural environment.

They weren't perfect and still made mistakes, but what they were very good at was quick solutions and prevention of issues before they became destroyers of civilisations.

Healthcare was benevolent, medicines complementary. Chemical based drugs, particularly those which affected mental thought processes, or consciousness were abhorred and outlawed by most civilisations in the galaxy.

Polluting fuel sources, waste, war and many other 'young' civilisation problems were virtually non-existent.

And so as humans brought these issues, they at first bemused the more advanced civilisations, then worried them, and then scared them.

Humans wouldn't think of the population before the self, the community before the individual.

And no amount of careful explanation or education from their peaceful mentors helped.

Humanity brought neither peace nor harmony, they brought intolerance and disrespect and selfishness.

Humanity's problem intensified when colonist ships became refugee ships as the Earth's biosphere collapsed. Now the ships didn't carry people looking to create an interplanetary civilisation as a first goal - they carried people who would be happy with any planet, any home, any port in the biggest storm ever faced by human civilisation.

And in this very moment, humanity's problem was one man's problem - no wonder Captain Delamonte looked haggard and stressed.

His ship was running out of supplies, and messages to and from other ships in the fleet were delivering the same reply - no one wants us!

This was going to require a rethink.

If no populated planet wanted them, where would they go?

How would the human race survive?

What was the answer?

# About the Author

Hunter Leonard is an author, speaker and business owner. He has a passion for helping business owners and mature individuals wanting to be more productive and prosperous.

After completing a botany degree at Macquarie University, Hunter entered the corporate world at a young age in a pharmaceutical sales role.

He transitioned into a marketing role, and has since built a successful career and then two successful businesses.

Hunter is curious about life and has a wide ranging portfolio of hobbies and interests including cooking, music, photography and bush walking.

Hunter and his wife—Nicole—divide their time between Melbourne and Sydney in supporting their two businesses.

Genetech P.S. is Hunter's first science fiction book.
You can connect with Hunter on his Linkedin page—https://www.

linkedin.com/in/hunter-leonard/